ONLY JOKING

Gabriel Josipovici was born in Nice in 1940 and lived in Egypt from 1945 to 1956, when he came to Britain. He read English at Oxford and taught at the University of Sussex from 1963 to 1996. His work includes fiction, drama and criticism, and has been widely translated.

'Whereas most great literature calls on *gravitas* to give it authority, the weighty burden of hefty concerns, strenuously raised, Josipovici fuels his narratives with *celeritas*, the playful swiftness of sleight of hand . . . Josipovici produces works that are cunning, intricate and elusive. Written almost entirely in fast-flowing streams of dialogue, they cut to the quick of what is lively and alive in both people and in narrative, the world of oral storytelling encapsulated in swarming vibrancy on the printed page . . . There is no one else like him.'
  – Victoria Best, *Tales from the Reading Room*

also by Gabriel Josipovici

GABRIEL JOSIPOVICI

Only Joking

ⒷB *editions*

I am grateful to George Szirtes for introducing me to the poetry of Sándor Petöfi and allowing me to use his translation of the poem which appears on page 84.

First published in Germany in 2006
under the title *Nur ein Scherz*
by Gerd Haffmans Bei Zweitausendeins
This edition first published in Great Britain in 2010
by CB editions
146 Percy Road London W12 9QL
www.cbeditions.com

Printed in England by Blissetts, London W3 8DH

ISBN 978-0-9561073-6-7

for David

I

When the Baron, as he likes to be called, wants to talk, he always sits in the front. Felix, at the wheel, knows better than to initiate a conversation. He busies himself manoeuvring the large silent car through the congested streets of Henley.

It is not till they are approaching the motorway that the Baron speaks.

– Miss Jenkin was in her usual excellent form, he says.

– I am glad to hear it, sir, Felix says, as he always does when the Baron imparts this item of information after his weekly visit.

– Her memory of my childish misdemeanours was sharper even than usual, the Baron says. I sometimes think she makes up these stories solely in order to make me squirm.

Felix smiles, his eyes on the road.

– To listen to her, the Baron says, you would think I had spent my entire youth in an effort to make life as miserable as possible for those whose company I was forced to keep.

The Baron is silent for so long after this that Felix, his eyes on the road and the rear-view mirror, might have been forgiven for thinking he had gone to sleep.

– And yet she seems to bear me no grudge, the Baron finally resumes, as though he had not paused at all. Quite the reverse, in fact. In her memory my escapades and practical jokes become the signs of a loveable zest, a charming independence of spirit.

The Baron lapses once more into silence.

– At least, he resumes after a while, that is how she appears to want me to imagine she looks back at my youthful self. At the same time she seems to suggest by her demeanour that this is the view of an overindulgent and slightly senile old lady, and that quite a different interpretation of my behaviour is not only possible but quite likely.

– The question I keep asking myself, the Baron says, is whether she is conscious of this or not, whether she wants me to draw this inference from her manner and remarks or it is only my guilty conscience which makes me do so.

Felix, his face impassive, steers the big car soundlessly past the rest of the traffic on the outside lane.

– Felix, the Baron says, there is something I have been meaning to ask you.

– Yes sir? Felix says.

– Felix, the Baron says, would you, with your extensive acquaintance, happen to know of someone who might be able to help me?

His eyes on the road, Felix waits for him to continue.

– A friend of mine, the Baron says, is looking for someone, a reliable man, to tail someone for him. Would you happen to know of such a man?

Felix gives no sign of having heard. The Baron, however, is content to wait.

Finally Felix says: I believe I do, sir.

– A reliable man?

– He does things in his own way, Felix says. He should be left to do them in his own way, if you understand me, sir.

– I am sure my friend would not dream of dictating to him, the Baron says. Perhaps you would be so kind, Felix, as to leave me his name and telephone number when we get home.

– I will be happy to do so, sir, Felix says as he guides the big car off the motorway and heads towards Highgate.

The Baron sighs and looks at his watch. – Five o'clock, he says. Sports report.

Felix leans forward and switches on the radio.

– The person in question, Mr Alphonse, is my wife, the Baron says.

– Just Alphonse, the man says.

They are sitting on a bench overlooking the river, between Westminster and Lambeth Bridge, on a cold spring day.

– Everybody calls me Alphonse, the man says.

The Baron acknowledges this with a little smile.

– The lady lives with you? Alphonse asks.

– In a manner of speaking, the Baron says. In a manner of speaking.

He produces a photo from his wallet and hands it to Alphonse, who studies it in silence.

– What else do you need to know? the Baron asks.

– I would appreciate a timetable of the lady's movements, Alphonse says.

– A timetable?

– Only as a rough guide, you understand.

– If that is what you require, of course, the Baron says.

Alphonse goes on scrutinising the photo. A helicopter passes overhead, following the river southwards.

– Slightly flattering, the Baron says. She's very photogenic. Always was. In real life she shows her age.

– Which is? Alphonse asks, still gazing at the photo.

– Fifty-four, the Baron says. Or thereabouts.

– I see, Alphonse says. A handsome woman, he opines,

swivelling round on the bench to look at the Baron, who goes on staring at the river.

– May I? Alphonse asks finally, holding up the photo.

– Of course, the Baron says. That is why I brought it.

Alphonse puts it carefully away in his wallet.

An envelope materialises in the Baron's hand. – As I am sure you realise, he says, there must be the minimum of contact between us. Inside you will find, as well as the advance agreed on, my mobile number followed by my home number. Please destroy them as soon as you have memorised them. You will only use them in an emergency. My wife is extremely suspicious. She must not have the slightest inkling that anything is going on. I will ring you regularly to find out how you are progressing but you will only ring me in an emergency. Is that understood?

Alphonse slips the envelope, unopened, into his jacket pocket. – These things take time, as you will appreciate, he says. First of all there is –

– Spare me the details, please, the Baron says, laying a hand on his arm.

– As you wish, Alphonse says, a note of disappointment in his voice.

– I am not in a hurry, the Baron says. What I need is firm evidence.

Alphonse draws his dark overcoat tight around him.

– She has always been a little eccentric, the Baron says. A little – how shall I say? – lacking in awareness of the unspoken rules that regulate social behaviour. In recent months, however, I have had the feeling that she was starting to lose control of herself. And now I have reason to believe that she is seeing another man.

Now it is Alphonse's turn to gaze out at the river.

– I must confess I was surprised, the Baron says. She has never evinced any interest in men or sex, only in money.

– Perhaps the man has money, Alphonse ventures.

– I doubt if he has as much as I have, the Baron says. I have taken the liberty, he goes on, of glancing at her diary. She seems to be plotting with this man, or to imagine that she is plotting with this man, to kill someone. If that is indeed the case, I would want to save her from herself. If I am to be the victim, I would naturally want to save myself. All that needs to be investigated. Who is the man? Is he her lover or an accomplice or both? Who is the intended victim, if indeed there is one? And so on. Do you understand?

– Of course, Alphonse says.

– That is why, when I say I am not in a hurry, the Baron says, it does not mean that we have unlimited time. If we are to save her from herself. And others.

– I quite understand, Alphonse says.

– I think that is all, the Baron says. Where do you wish me to send the timetable?

– You could write it out now, Alphonse says. It would save trouble. It really would.

The Baron brings a little notebook with gold corners and a gold-tipped pen out from an inner pocket. He crosses his legs, hitching up his trousers to save the crease, and opens the notebook on his knee. Alphonse takes out a crumpled packet of cigarettes, selects one, lights it, and inhales with relish.

– I would rather you didn't smoke in my presence, the Baron says, without looking up.

Alphonse takes the cigarette out of his mouth, examines

[6]

it, then flicks it into the river. He takes out the envelope the Baron has just given him, opens it, counts the money, returns the envelope to his jacket pocket.

– There you are, the Baron says, tearing a sheet out of his notebook and handing it to him. Alphonse glances at it.

– I will study it at my leisure, he says, slipping it into his wallet next to the photograph.

– Is there anything else you need to know? the Baron asks.

– No, Alphonse says. I think I have enough to be going on with.

– Good, the Baron says. He stands up. I will be in touch with you a week from now, he says.

– A great deal of patience is required from all parties in matters of this kind, Alphonse says.

– Quite so, the Baron says. Good day to you.

He sets off in the direction of Lambeth Bridge. Above him the gulls wheel and screech.

Alphonse takes the packet of cigarettes out again, selects one, puts in it his mouth, lights it and, leaning back on the bench, closes his eyes as he slowly exhales.

3

Elspeth, in a purple dress and matching hat with peacock feather at a jaunty angle, is entertaining Alphonse in one of her favourite restaurants, Xavier's in Marylebone High Street.

– He has been *taken over* by these people, Alphonse, she says. They have *warped his mind*. They have made *strangers* of us. When he looks at me now, she says, it's as if I was something the cat had brought in. And whenever we meet they positively *gloat*. Alphonse, she says, when are you going to *act*?

She lights a cigarette from the butt of the one she is smoking and then crushes the butt out fiercely in the overflowing ashtray. A waiter materialises out of nowhere, and with a single gesture removes the ashtray and substitutes a clean one, then vanishes again.

– You smoke too much, Elspeth, Alphonse says. You really do.

– When, Alphonse? she says, tossing back the feather. When?

– The Baron got in touch with me last week, Alphonse says quietly.

– The Baron?

– Yes, Alphonse says. He really did.

– The Baron? she says again. Why?

– He wished to employ me, Alphonse says.

— Employ you? she says. But he can't. I'm employing you already.

— He doesn't know that, Alphonse says.

— You didn't tell him?

Alphonse leans across the table. — He wants me to tail you, he says quietly.

— To tail me?

— Yes.

— What does that mean, Alphonse? she says, growing pale beneath her make-up.

— It means follow you, Elspeth, he says. It means look into your affairs and see what you are up to.

— Oh, she says, laughing wildly. I thought it was like topped and tailed.

— He thinks, Alphonse says, lowering his voice, that you are seeing another man.

— Me? she says.

— You know, Alphonse says, as the waiter wheels the dessert trolley forward, I think I would rather like some of that crème caramel.

— With cream, sir?

— Why not? Alphonse says.

They wait while the man goes about his business.

— And for madame? he asks.

— I'll just have coffee, Victor, Elspeth says. And a brandy.

— For me as well, Alphonse says.

— Coffee or brandy, sir?

— Both, Alphonse says. Both.

When he has gone she leans across the table and says to Alphonse: Look at that man! Look at him slouching in his chair! It's disgraceful!

– Elspeth, Alphonse says.

– Waiter! she calls. And, when he has come: A piece of paper and a pen, Victor, please.

– Elspeth, Alphonse says. Did you hear what I said?

– It's disgraceful, she says. I can't bear to see people slumped in their chairs like that. It's bad for their backs. It's bad for *my* back just seeing him.

She scribbles, folds the sheet in four and hands it to the waiter. – Please give it to the gentleman there in the corner.

– The gentleman?

– That man there. Slumped in his chair.

– Very good, madame.

– Elspeth, Alphonse says. Listen to me, will you?

– In a minute, Alphonse, in a minute.

She watches intently as the man opens the missive with the waiter hovering in attendance. He glances at her, folds it again, puts it in his pocket and resumes his conversation with his friend.

– It's for his own good, she says. He'll be bedridden before he's sixty if he goes on like that.

– Elspeth, Alphonse says. I wish you would concentrate on what I am telling you and not draw attention to yourself like that.

The coffee and brandy arrive. Elspeth lights another cigarette. Alphonse pushes his empty dessert bowl aside and draws the coffee cup to him. – He thinks you're seeing another man, he says again.

– Rubbish, Elspeth says. He knows me better than that.

– You aren't?

– It's none of your business if I am, Elspeth says. But as it happens I'm not.

– Think about it, Alphonse says, smiling. He raises his brandy glass to his nose and closes his eyes as he inhales.

Light dawns on her. – You mean you? she says.

He smiles at her over the rim of the glass.

– Ridiculous, she says.

– It's the truth, he says. From his point of view. It really is.

– But how did he –? What . . .?

– He found your diary and read it, Alphonse says. I told you to be more discreet.

– He couldn't have, she says. I'm as discreet as could be. Besides, it's in code.

Alphonse sips his brandy.

– Alphonse, she says. Do you think he knows about our plan?

Alphonse shrugs.

– But why you? she says, struck by a sudden thought. Why did he approach you of all people with this . . . tailing?

– Felix recommended me, Alphonse says, smiling at her.

– He couldn't have, she says. He recommended you to *me*.

She takes out her compact, applies lipstick, snaps the compact shut and lights another cigarette. Soundlessly, a waiter removes the ashtray and in one movement substitutes a clean one.

– Felix has confidence in me, Alphonse says. He knows I'm good.

– I don't care if he knows everything, she says. He's not going to stop me.

– He's only guessing, Alphonse says. For the moment he wants me to tail you and find out more.

– You can't be sure with him, she says. He never gives anything away.

– *I* can be sure, Alphonse says. I really can.

– What are you going to do? she asks.

– Do?

– What are you going to tell him, Alphonse? And stop smiling like that, I can't stand it when you smile.

– I shall report to him, Alphonse says, going on smiling at her over the rim of his glass. I shall keep him informed. Meanwhile, we will proceed as planned.

– Alphonse, she says, the quicker you get this done the better. I told you it was urgent.

– Elspeth, he says. I've explained to you. These things take time. They cannot be done in a day.

– You've had time, Alphonse, she says. You've had time and you've had money. I want to see some results now.

– It won't do to rush it, Alphonse says. Not a job like this. It really won't.

– That's what you keep saying, she says.

– And why do I keep saying it? Because it's the truth, Elspeth. It really is.

– Oh, Alphonse, she says. I'm so frightened. What if he knows our plans? What if he's only waiting to pounce?

– Calm yourself, Elspeth, he says. Leave everything to me.

– I have left it to you, she says. And look what's happened. Nothing.

– You know what the secret of being a good clown is, Elspeth? he asks.

– No, she says. You've told me but I've forgotten.

– Innocence, Elspeth, he says. A clown is innocent. He is innocent because he has not been born into our world. He is innocent, Elspeth, because he has not been born at all.

– I don't know what you're trying to tell me, Alphonse,

she says. You confuse me with all your words. We don't have much time left, Alphonse, she says. You've got to act now if you're going to act at all.

— I'm making my plans, Elspeth, Alphonse says. I really am.

— That's what you keep saying.

— And why do I keep saying it?

— How should I know? she says.

— It's because it's the truth, Elspeth. It really is.

— We shouldn't be seen together, she says. I don't know why we meet like this in public.

— It was your suggestion, he says.

— Well we're not doing anything wrong, she says, tossing back her feather. I can eat with who I like, can't I?

— Yes, Elspeth, he says.

— He may have seen us together, she says. You don't know what he's like. Don't be taken in by his charm, Alphonse.

— Calm yourself, Elspeth, he says. Please calm yourself.

— I'm perfectly calm, she says. What are you going to tell him?

— Who?

— The Baron.

— What about him?

— What are you going to tell him about me? About me seeing another man?

The two men in the corner get up. A waiter helps them on with their coats. As he goes out the one to whom she has sent the note purses his lips and wags a finger at her. She lights another cigarette from the butt before stubbing the butt out fiercely in the ashtray.

— I'll think of something, Alphonse says. I really will.

4

– I'm tired, Lino, Alphonse says. These people tire me out. They really do.

– No problem, Lino says. Let me get you a coffee and you'll feel better.

They are sitting in the back room, behind Lino's restaurant in Knightsbridge. Lino brings him an espresso and sits in silence while he sips it.

Lino's daughter, Rosalia, comes in. Her father embraces her. – Have you eaten yet, *cara*? he asks her.

– Yes.

– Where?

– Never mind, she says.

She throws herself down on the sofa and closes her eyes.

– Not as good as you could eat here, her father says. Why you never eat here?

She lies on the sofa, eyes closed.

– Why, *cara*? he says. Why?

– Leave me alone, Papa.

Lino turns back to Alphonse. – How you doing, then? he asks.

– Look, Alphonse says. He pulls a wad of notes from his breast pocket and flashes it at Lino.

Lino whistles.

– Now I work for him *and* for her, Alphonse says.

– You don't say? How you do it?

– I have my methods, Alphonse says. I really do.

– And each pay you to keep watch on the other?

– More or less.

– You're a clever one, Alphonse, Lino says.

– There's more to come, Alphonse says. Two thirds when I deliver for her, half when I deliver for him.

– And you deliver?

– I have my methods, Alphonse says.

The girl gets up from the sofa with a sigh.

– How's Rosie? Alphonse says, as her father embraces her.

– OK.

– Still an artist?

– Art student.

– What's the difference?

– Work it out, smart-ass.

– Hey, Lino says. Watch your language.

– One day perhaps I commission you to do my portrait, Alphonse says.

– Yeah yeah, she says. Dream on.

– I live on dreams, Alphonse says.

The notes reappear in his hand, spread fanwise. – You want to see a trick?

– Go on.

– You're looking?

– Yeah yeah. Get on with it.

– OK. One two three, and away they go.

She scratches her head.

– Where did they go, my sweet? Alphonse asks.

– How should I know?

– You want me to show you?

– OK.

– There they are, my chick, Alphonse says, reaching out and fishing them from her coat pocket. Good, eh? he says.

– OK.

– I got a lot more where that came from, Alphonse says. A whole lot more.

– Cash or tricks?

– Both, my chick, both.

She turns away from him. – I'm going, Papa, she says.

– Where, *cara*?

– Don't always ask me questions, Papa.

– Are you going to the college?

– I told you, she says. Don't always ask me questions.

– She didn't think much of my trick, Alphonse says when she has gone.

– She's seen it before.

– Not with fifties. Not with fifty fifties.

– Money don't interest her, Lino says. Only men.

– I'm a man, Alphonse says.

– You keep away from my daughter, Lino says.

– Hey, Alphonse says. Only joking.

– Me too, Lino says.

5

– So, in the last scene, Charlie says, there's this big shoot-out, but the camera doesn't move. Sometimes the characters come into shot, sometimes not, sometimes you just hear things and there's nothing at all on the screen except this clearing in the woods and the sounds of the birds and a tree creaking somewhere and –

– I don't get it, Natasha says.

Rosie, out of breath, flops down at their table. – Hi, she says.

A waiter appears. – Macchiato, she says. She tells the others: You remember that guy I told you about? The clown?

– What clown?

– This friend of my dad's. He was in the back today, showing my dad this wad of money.

– How much?

– Shitloads. Fifties. He's doing a couple of jobs and they've paid him the advances.

– He keeps it on him?

– He likes to flash it around. He does a trick with the notes, spreading them out like a pack of cards and then making them disappear and finding them again in your coat pocket, that sort of thing.

– He did it to you?

– Yeah.

– You should've skipped before he pulled them out.

— Yeah yeah.

— You know him?

— I told you about him. He's a friend of my dad's. Tall. Heavy. Quite a good looker. Little trimmed beard. His name's Alphonse.

— Alphonse?

— He used to be a clown. That's his clown's name.

— It's a funny name for a clown.

— I don't know. He's foreign.

— He's often in with your dad?

— Yeah. Now and then.

— What kind of work does he do?

— Tails people, I think.

— You sure it was fifties?

— Yeah. He pulled them out of his pocket.

— You think he's on the video?

— Could be. He's in and out of there. I don't like him though.

Her coffee arrives. She gets up to find an ashtray, begins to talk to the people at the next table.

— So when this guy's killed, Charlie says, you see the blood just sort of seeping onto the screen. You hear the thump of the bullet and the heavier thump of a body falling and then after a while you just see the blood seeping onto the screen from the right, seeping over the grass. And then, very slowly, a hand, and then a bit of an arm.

— It sounds pretty crappy to me, Natasha says.

Rosie comes back to their table. — I've got to try and find some shoes, she says. Will you guys be here for a while?

— Could be, Charlie says.

— I'll look in, Rosie says, swallowing her coffee and leaving a coin on the table.

When she has gone Charlie says: Well?

– Well what?

– Shall we go for it?

– For the clown?

– Uhuh.

– Why not?

– I find it distasteful, Charlie says, that someone like that should have so much paper. I think we owe it to society to relieve him of some of it. Liberty, fraternity *and equality* was what the man said, after all. Do you think you can do it?

– Easy peasy, Natasha says.

– He could be dangerous.

– He sounds pretty pleased with himself, she says. People who are pleased with themselves are rarely dangerous.

– How long do you think you'll need?

– It depends, doesn't it?

– I'm not sure I like it.

– Why not?

– I don't like the idea of you in the same flat with this guy.

– Shit, she says. I can take care of myself.

– You'll have to be careful.

– Hey! she says, I am careful.

– OK, he says. Let's give it a go.

– How do we find him?

– I'll have a look at the video, he says. And I'll get on to Rosie.

– You're going to tell her?

– There's no need, he says. But if he's a regular at the restaurant we should be able to work something out.

6

The smartly dressed man with neatly trimmed beard sheltering under the awning of a Knightsbridge restaurant stretches out an arm and pulls a tall young woman out of the drizzle and into the shelter of the awning.

– Awah! she says. Let me go!

– You'll get wet, he says, not releasing her. You really will.

– Let me go, she says. I'll call the police.

– No you won't, he says. Not with that in your pocket.

– What do you mean? she says. Nevertheless, she ceases to struggle and for a while the two of them stand side by side under the awning, contemplating the wet pavements and the pedestrians hurrying by.

Finally she says: What do you know about it?

– I saw you, he says. I admired your style.

She is silent for a while, as she appears to digest this piece of information. Then she says: You want it?

He squeezes her arm. – Call me Alphonse, he says.

She puts her hand in her coat pocket.

– No no, he says. Please.

– What do you want, then?

– Why don't we talk? he says. There are things we could do together, you and I, there really are.

– What sort of things?

– Business, he says. You and I could do business together. We really could.

– What makes you think I want to do business with you? she says.

– This makes me think, he says, patting her pocket. Why don't we go and have a coffee and talk?

•

In the café he looks into her eyes. – What's your name? he asks.

– Isabelle, Natasha says.

– It's a beautiful name.

He holds out his hand.

– What? she says.

– Give.

– No.

– Come on, Isabelle. I want to see what's in it.

– No, she says.

– Why don't you have a look yourself?

She takes the wallet out of her coat pocket, pulls out a wad of notes, flashes them at him.

He whistles. – You're a clever girl, Isabelle.

She examines the wallet.

– Credit cards? he asks.

– Nix.

– Silly bugger, he says.

She returns the wallet to her coat pocket.

– All right, he says. You keep it. You earned it.

– What's that funny accent you have? she asks.

– I haven't got a funny accent.

– What is it?

– Hungarian.

– Hungarian?

– I'm Hungarian.

– With a name like that?

– It's my professional name, he says.

– What profession?

– Clown.

– Ah, Natasha says, appraising him with her large blue eyes.

– It's an ancient and honourable profession, he says. Perhaps the most ancient in the world.

– Look, she says, what are you proposing?

– I have a spare room, he says. Nice flat. I could put you up. We could work together.

– Where?

– Kennington.

– That doesn't sound very nice, she says.

– It's a nice flat, he says. Gives on to a nice square. Plenty of trees. What about it?

– Maybe, she says.

– Make it yes or no, he says.

– I'll need to pick up my gear.

– Where from?

– Not far from here.

– I'll come with you, he says.

– What for?

– I don't want you to disappear.

– I don't want to disappear.

– That's good, he says. I have plans for the two of us, Isabelle. I really do.

– So do I, Natasha says.

– What do you do, Isabelle?

– I'm an art student.

– I know an art student. Name of Rosie.

– London's a big place, she says.

– Let's go, he says.

– OK, she says. But you'll have to wait outside. My boy-friend wouldn't like it if he was to see the two of us together.

– Your boyfriend is of no interest to me, Isabelle, he says.

– He's not of much interest to me, she says. We just work together.

– What sort of work?

– Art work, she says. He's beautiful but he's a pain in the ass.

– You get your things and get out of there, Alphonse says. I'll wait outside.

•

Charlie is lying on the bed listening to the White Stripes. She tosses the wallet over to him. – I've got to work fast, she says. He's waiting for me round the corner.

– He bought it?

– I told you, she says. Easy peasy.

– What's he like?

– OK, she says, pulling a suitcase from under the bed and starting to stuff it with clothes.

– Sure you can handle him?

– Of course.

– When will you call me?

– When I'm done.

She sits on the suitcase and zips it shut.

– No, he says. I want to know how it's going.

– What's the point? she says.

She goes into the bathroom and begins to apply her make-up.

– What's that supposed to mean? he says, standing at the door.

She pushes her washing things into a bag.

– You're not getting any ideas, are you, Tash?

– What do you mean?

– You know what I mean, he says.

He watches her. – Remember, he says. We're in this together, Tash.

– Oh fuck off, she says, pushing past him.

– I just want you to remember, he says, standing firm.

– Get out of the way, she says. He's waiting.

He bars her way. – Tash, he says.

– Oh fuck off!

– All right, he says, stepping back. See you then.

– And you, she says, picking up her bag and suitcase and making for the door.

•

– This, Alphonse says, standing back, is your room.

– This?

– You don't like it?

– I'll have to think about it.

She goes to the window and looks down into the tree-filled square below.

– It's a nice room, Isabelle, he says. Nice spot.

– There's too much furniture in it.

– What do you mean?

– I'm a big girl, Natasha says. I need room to move about.

– I'll make room, Isabelle, I really will.

– What's this? she says.

– My accordion, he says.

– You play the accordion?

– I do, he says.

– I thought accordions went out with the toaster.

– Every Hungarian plays the accordion, Alphonse says.

– You'll have to get it out of here, she says. And that silly table. I'm a big girl. I don't want to keep banging into the furniture the whole time.

– Where am I going to put it? he says. You've seen the size of the flat.

– That's your problem, she says.

– It will be done, my poppet, he says. It really will.

7

– Can I speak to Alphonse please?

– I'm afraid he's not at home.

– Who is that please?

– A friend.

– I see . . .

– Can I give him a message?

– No. I'll call back.

– Who shall I say called?

There is a silence. Then: Tell him the Baron. I need to speak to him urgently.

– Of course.

– Goodbye, then.

– Goodbye, Natasha says.

•

Turning out of the square in the direction of the Underground, she suddenly finds her arm gripped from behind.

– Awah! she says, twisting round to see who her assailant is and finding herself staring into Charlie's pale, handsome face.

– What the hell are you doing here?

– What do you think? he says.

– Awah! she says again as he lets her arm go. You hurt me, you brute!

– Sorry, he says

– How did you find me?

– I followed you.

– When?

– The other day.

– You're spying on me, you shit.

– You were going to ring me, he says. Remember?

She shakes her arm. – You hurt me, you bastard.

She starts to walk again. He falls into step beside her. – You were going to ring me, he says. Why didn't you?

– You're spying on me, she says. I hate that. I hate it. I hate it.

– What's happened? he says. Why haven't you been in touch?

– There isn't anything to report.

– You haven't found anything?

– Of course I haven't. Why do you think I'm still here?

– You could have let me know, he says.

– Look, she says, we worked all this out beforehand. Do you want to ruin it all? Because you will if he catches us together.

– What've you told him?

– Nothing.

– About us, I mean.

– Nothing.

– You're not sleeping with him, are you, Tash?

– It's none of your business.

– You are?

– I told you. It's none of your business.

– Tash, he says, you wouldn't do that to me, would you?

– Fuck off, she says. You're not funny.

– Would you?

– It's not funny, Charlie, she says.

– I need to know, he says.

– Nothing's happened.

– You could have rung and told me.

– What would have been the point?

– You said you would.

– I said I'd let you know if I needed you.

– As soon as you found anything.

– Well I haven't yet.

– It's probably in the bank by now.

– No. He's shown me the trick.

– The one with the notes?

– Uhuh.

– So he keeps the stuff on him. But hides it somewhere.

– Bright boy, she says.

– It's not a big place, is it? he says. It shouldn't take long to find.

– Look, she says, you'll ruin everything if he sees you here.

– He won't recognise me without the whiskers.

– That's not the point, she says. We made a plan. Why don't you bloody stick to it? Why do you have to follow us like that and spy on me?

– The plan included your getting in touch, he says. Letting me know how it was going. We're in this together, Tash, remember.

– You think I'm going to skip with the paper?

– I just think you should keep me informed. I don't know what the hell is going on.

– Why did you follow me? she says. It wasn't part of the arrangement.

– You promise you're not sleeping with him?

– That's my business, she says.

– Mine too, he says.

– How do you work that out?

– Well, he says, isn't it?

– Not any more, she says.

– Why not?

– Because you spy on me, that's why.

– So you are.

– What?

– Sleeping with him.

– Of course.

– I don't believe you.

– Then why do you ask?

She quickens her step. He takes her arm again. She shakes it off.

– Is that all you've got to say? he says.

– Oh fuck off, she says.

– OK, he says. OK. But you'll get in touch when you have something concrete?

– Not if you spy on me, she says. I'll never forgive you for that.

– *Force majeure*, he says, trying to sound light-hearted. *Force majeure.*

But she has already turned the corner.

•

He finds Rosie sitting at the back of the restaurant with the rest of the family.

– Fancy a film? he asks, after the greetings.

– Sure, she says. Why not?

– You were going to eat with us, her mother says to her. Why don't you stay too, Charlie?

– Don't tempt me, Patrizia.

– Why not? Temptation is good.

– Not for my figure.

– Figure? she says. Figure? At your age you don't have to think of your figure.

– I'm getting into practice for when I do.

– How's the filming then, Charlie? Lino asks him.

– They're not films, Lino.

– You know what I mean, Charlie.

– Sure, sure.

– One day you show me your films, eh? I want to see the one you made of the door.

– It didn't work out.

– What do you mean, it didn't work out?

– I didn't like it.

– How can you like it? Lino says. A camera filming a door for one week. Is that something you like? Is the people not good enough for you, then?

– What people?

– The people who go in and out.

– Maybe, Charlie says.

– You don't understand, Papa, Rosie says.

– Why? Because I'm not clever enough? Because I don't have art training?

– That's right, Lino, Charlie says.

– So you only understand if you have art training? Is that what you're telling me, Charlie?

– He's having you on, Papa, Rosie says.

– It just didn't work out, Lino, Charlie says. That's all there is to it.

– Charlie's having a show soon, Papa, Rosie says. Aren't you, Charlie?

– Uhuh, Charlie says.

– Send me an invitation, Lino says. I love the movies.

– I don't make movies.

– I know I know. But you know what I mean.

– Sure I'll send you an invitation, Lino, Charlie says. And now we have to go.

8

— May I speak to Alphonse, please?

— I'm afraid Alphonse is not at home.

— Who is that, please?

— A friend.

— Are you living there?

— I'm sorry?

— I understood that Alphonse lived on his own?

— Yes, Natasha says. He lives on his own.

— Is that the cleaning lady I'm talking to?

— No, Natasha said. A friend.

— A close friend?

— What does close mean? Natasha asks.

There is a silence at the other end. Then the Baron says: Would you be so kind as to tell him the Baron called? It's urgent. Tell him it's urgent. Tell him to switch on his mobile. Ask him to ring me back as soon as possible.

— All that?

— No. Just the last bit.

— No probs, Natasha says.

— I beg your pardon?

— I'll give him your message.

— Thank you. Goodbye.

She puts down the phone and returns to her labours.

The phone rings again.

— On second thoughts, the Baron says, he'd better not

phone me. Can you tell me when he'll be in?

    – I've no idea, Natasha says.

    – Can you tell him I'll phone tomorrow before nine?

    – He sleeps till nine, Natasha says.

    – Good, the Baron says. I'll wake him up.

9

Elspeth, in an elaborate brown wool dress and with a brown bow in her hair, is taking Alphonse out to lunch in one of her favourite restaurants, the Torquato Tasso in Covent Garden.

– The time has come to act, Alphonse says.

– I should hope so indeed, Elspeth says. I paid you a great deal of money to carry out a specific task and so far all you've done is eat my food and talk sweetly to me.

– That's unfair, Elspeth, Alphonse says. It really is. It's unfair first of all because the food is not yours, second because it was you who suggested that we have lunch together, and third because sweet talk is better than bitter talk.

– There you go again, Elspeth says, lighting a cigarette from the butt and crushing the butt out in the overflowing ashtray.

A waiter materialises, deftly substitutes a clean ashtray for the dirty one, and disappears again.

– I would like you to introduce me to them, Alphonse says, smiling at her across the table.

– To whom?

– To them.

– Who's them?

– Them.

– Are you mad? she says.

Alphonse, his napkin under his chin, his little grey beard

very neatly trimmed, tucks into his pasta. — There are very few people, he says, who know how to make a simple Neapolitan spaghetti dish. They either try too hard or they do not try hard enough. Only a first-rate cook will get it exactly right, and when it is not exactly right it is completely wrong. Like the piano music of Anton Webern.

— Are you mad? she says again.

— Why mad?

— Surely, she says, in cases like this, the less contact there is between the . . . and the . . .

— Elspeth, Elspeth, he says, you have been reading too many thrillers. You really have.

— But it stands to reason, she says. The less there is to connect me to you and you to them the less likely they are to pin anything on either of us.

— Why then are you having lunch with me, Elspeth? Alphonse says. Why did we have lunch last week and the week before that and the week before that?

— I knew it was madness, she says. But I had to see you. I had to find out what was happening. Oh, Alphonse, she says, I'm so frightened and confused.

— It isn't madness, Alphonse says, stretching an arm out across the stiff white tablecloth and laying his hand on hers. You're always so melodramatic, Elspeth. You have hired me to do a job. Would you have hired me if you didn't feel I could do it? Would I have accepted if I did not think I could do it?

— I hired you because Felix recommended you, she says.

— And would Felix have recommended me if he thought I didn't know how to do my job?

— I told him I had a friend who needed someone to frighten

[35]

some people, she says. I didn't tell him it was for me and that frightening meant killing.

– Shshshshshsh, he says. Shshshshshsh. We all know what frightening means, Elspeth. We really do.

– Alphonse, she says. I want action. The baby is due any time now and then it will be too late. You don't know what they're like, she says, the way they *humiliate* me, the way they *sneer* at me. They know that when the Baron dies I will be a *pauper*, Alphonse, a *pauper*. Alphonse, have you any conception of what that means? Have you any –?

– Elspeth, Elspeth, he says. You are getting over-excited. There is plenty of time. Plenty of time. And when I carry out my little plan, he says, there will be nothing to connect me to you or you to it. You need have no fear, Elspeth. In the meantime it would be helpful to see inside the house. I need to get a sense of these two people and how they live.

– I don't like it, she says, lighting a fresh cigarette.

– Do you like any of this?

– Oh, Alphonse, she says, I'm so frightened. What's going to become of me?

– Elspeth, he says, set your mind at rest. You are paying me so as to have your mind set at rest, so why should you try to do my job at the same time?

– Do you have to meet them? she asks.

– I really do, he says.

– Isn't that sort of thing better done if one knows nothing about the people one . . .

– Elspeth, Alphonse says, laying a hand on her arm again. Elspeth.

– It has to be this way? she says.

– It really does, he says.

She thinks about it. – Maybe I can arrange something, she says. Are you fond of art, Alphonse?

– Me? Alphonse says. I'm an artist myself, Elspeth. Sometimes you seem to forget that.

– I mean painting.

– All art springs from the same source, Elspeth. When I was growing up on Lake Balaton there was no art on the wall, no galleries, no sculpture in the parks, no arts councils and artists in residence, no poetry readings and Turner Prizes. We were all artists. The women who wove the baskets, the men who ploughed the fields, the children who played games. My father, he says, was a wonderful man. An illiterate peasant, perhaps, but he could carve a piece of wood, a branch cut from a tree, so that you felt the figure was alive, more alive than you were. My mother –

– I thought your father was a banker? she says.

– Later, he says. Later he became a banker. He really did.

– Giles is something of a collector, she says. He recently acquired a Braque. He paid four million for it. Can you believe it? Four million? I could live off that for the rest of my life and to hell with the Baron, and he spends it on a painting.

– Braque is one of my favourite painters, Alphonse says. Roped together on the steep slope of Parnassus.

– What?

– What Picasso is supposed to have said of his collaboration with Braque in the Cubist years. We were two mountaineers roped together on the steep slope of Parnassus.

– He said that?

– Elspeth, Alphonse says. I will bring a friend.

– A friend?

– A lady friend. It always looks better if there is a lady friend.

– It does?

– It really does, Elspeth.

– Then bring her along by all means.

– There is the advantage that she is an artist herself.

– Is she really?

– Braque is of course to her old hat.

– Old hat?

– Prehistory, Alphonse says. One with the dinosaurs.

– Prehistory? Elspeth says. Dinosaurs? What are you talking about, Alphonse?

– Art moves on, Elspeth, Alphonse says. It moves all the time. Like the staircase in the Underground. My friend belongs to today, and Braque? Yesterday? The day before perhaps? But of course a wonderful painter. I told you, one of my favourites.

The waiter arrives with the main course.

10

– May I speak to Alphonse, please?

– Speaking.

– Alphonse! Where the deuce have you been? Your mobile seems to be permanently off and you never return my calls. What's the meaning of this?

– Is that the Baron?

– Of course it's the Baron. Who do you think it is? Alphonse, what's the meaning of this?

– Of what, Baron?

– Of this silence, man, of this silence.

– I thought the arrangement was that you would phone me, Baron.

– I've been trying to do that for the past week, Alphonse, didn't you get my messages?

– Of course, Baron, of course.

– Well then.

– Well then what, Baron?

– Alphonse, who is that woman who answered my calls?

– A friend.

– She's staying with you?

– Temporarily.

– Didn't she say I'd asked you to phone?

– But Baron, the arrangement was that you should phone me, not me you. You were most firm on that topic.

– But if I can never get hold of you, man!

There is a silence at the other end.

— For all I knew, the Baron says, you'd simply taken the money and run.

— Run, Baron?

— You know what I mean.

— Baron, Baron, Alphonse says, didn't Felix recommend me? Would he recommend someone who would do a flit?

— Look, Alphonse, in the future I want you to return any call of mine if I say I want you to.

— Yes, Baron. And what about the lady?

— What lady?

— You said you didn't want to receive any calls at home and naturally I assumed that . . .

— Alphonse, the Baron says, let me make this quite clear once and for all. When I leave a message asking you to call on me, you call. Understood?

— Understood, Baron.

— I wanted to know how you're getting on, the Baron says.

— Baron, Alphonse says, I am sure you realise you are not my only client.

— I am well aware of that, Alphonse. Indeed, I would be rather concerned if I were. Nevertheless, I am *one* of your clients. I have paid you an advance, a sizeable advance. I need results.

— Leave it to me, Baron, Alphonse says. Leave it to me.

— I have left it to you, the Baron says.

— That's just as it should be, Alphonse says.

— This friend, the Baron says. Is she safe?

— Safe, Baron?

— I mean, can you trust her? Is it all right for me to say who I am?

[40]

– Perfectly, Baron. She takes no interest in these matters.

– And when do you think you will have something to report, Alphonse?

– These things take time, Baron, Alphonse says. As I think I explained to you. There is first of all the –

– Spare me the details, the Baron says. How much time?

– I thought you were in no immediate hurry, Baron? I thought what you wanted was results. Concrete results.

– Precisely, Alphonse. But I did also explain to you that –

– You will have results as soon as possible, Alphonse says.

– How soon is that?

– Baron, Baron, Alphonse says, don't make it difficult for me. Try to put yourself in my shoes. A profile has to be built up. We are not talking here about a single fact, we are talking about an entire profile.

– I don't want her profile, Alphonse, the Baron says. I've had more than enough of her profile. I want the facts.

– But what are the facts, Baron? Empty husks, believe me. Without interpretation they are nothing. What you need is a profile which will help interpret the facts. When I have the profile in place you will have it, Baron, rest assured.

– I don't know what you're talking about, Alphonse, the Baron says. I want to know if you've found anything yet.

– And you, Baron?

– Me?

– Have you noticed any change in her behaviour?

– I can't find her diary any more, the Baron says. I think she may suspect something. I hope you're being discreet, Alphonse.

– Baron, Baron, Alphonse says. I don't think you should tell me how to do my job, I really don't, any more than I would tell you how to do yours. I have to go now, Baron. It was lovely to talk to you and of course, as soon as I have anything to report I will let you know. Meanwhile, call me any time, day or night, I am always at your service, Baron.

— Damn, the Baron says as the phone goes dead.

11

Rosie and Natasha are having coffee in the King's Road.

– That prat Charlie, Natasha says, won't let me alone.

– He feels you've hurt him, Rosie says.

– He's such a prat, Natasha says.

– He told me you'd moved out.

– He spies on me, Natasha says. He's followed me right out to Kennington. He trains his bloody video camera on me when I don't even know he's there.

– Perhaps you need a break from each other, Rosie says.

– You're bloody right we do.

– He thinks you don't love him any more.

– I don't.

– He thinks you've taken up with someone else.

– He's such a prat, Natasha says.

– Have you?

– What?

– Taken up with someone else.

– Of course not.

– He says you've moved in with that Alphonse guy.

– It's only a business arrangement, Natasha says.

– He thinks it's more than that.

– He can think what he likes. He's a prat.

– Do you want me to tell him anything? Rosie says. I'm seeing him this evening.

– No, Natasha says. Just don't discuss me with him, right?

– I'll try, she says. But he won't talk about much else.

– Tell him to keep away from me, Natasha says. Tell him to keep his bloody camera to himself.

– His camera's his life, Rosie says.

– Tell him to live his life elsewhere.

– I'll try, Rosie says.

12

Elspeth, in a tight-fitting black dress, black velvet beret and with very red fingernails and lips, steps into the large car. Felix closes the door behind her and goes round to the front.

– Mr Giles', Elspeth says.

– Very good, madam.

– Go via South Kensington Tube station, will you, Felix. We are picking up some friends.

She unwraps a boiled sweet and pops it into her mouth, for the Baron will not allow her to smoke in the car. Then she closes her eyes and dozes as the car swishes its way down from Highgate to South Kensington.

At the station Alphonse, very smart in homburg and dark overcoat, is waiting at the kerb, Natasha beside him, a bright pink scarf wrapped round her shoulders.

– My painter friend, Alphonse says, as Elspeth lowers the window. Isabelle, he says, Elspeth.

– Sit in front with Felix, Elspeth says to him. Your friend can sit in the back with me.

– Alphonse did not make clear the precise nature of your relationship to him, she says to Natasha as the large car glides through the tree-lined streets.

– We're not related, Natasha says.

– I meant, Elspeth says, well, I'm not exactly sure what I meant, but it wasn't that.

– Isabelle advises me about the art world, Alphonse says, swivelling round in his seat.

– Surely Isabelle can speak for herself? Elspeth says. Can't you, dear?

– Of course, Natasha says.

– Tell me something about yourself, Elspeth says. I love hearing about other people's lives.

– Where do you want me to start? Natasha asks.

– Now, now, Elspeth says.

Felix keeps his eyes on the road and the rear-view mirror. Alphonse slumps beside him.

– Why not begin with what you do? Elspeth says.

– I'm an art student.

– And what kind of art do you study?

– I don't study it. I make it.

– What kind of art do you make, then?

– All kinds, Natasha says.

– Her work, Alphonse says, swivelling round once more, is mainly site-specific.

– What's that? asks Elspeth.

– He doesn't know what he's talking about, Natasha says.

– Then explain a little more please.

– I don't feel like it.

– Oh, Elspeth says, and, when the other remains silent: What, for example, is your current project?

– Tomorrow, Natasha says, if I feel like it, I might make a papier-mâché model of this car with all of us inside it just like we are now.

– Oh goodness, Elspeth says. Will you really?

– Only joking, Natasha says.

– I don't think I get the joke, Elspeth says.

– It doesn't matter.

– You won't explain it?

– It isn't a joke any more if you explain it.

– Even to a dimwit like me?

Felix pulls up at the kerb. – Here we are, madam, he says.

– I don't know how long we'll be, Elspeth says to him. Why don't you come back in an hour?

– Very good, madam.

– I must have a fag before we go in, Elspeth says, lighting up as they stand on the pavement. Can't smoke in the car, can't smoke at Giles'. It's time we had a revolution. Smokers of the world, unite!

Felix moves the car out into the traffic. Alphonse coughs and looks about him.

– There, Elspeth says, throwing the butt into the gutter. Let's go.

They follow her through the gate and up a few stairs to a smart front door, very blue. She rings and they wait.

A pale beauty, heavily pregnant, opens the door.

– Darling, Elspeth says.

They embrace.

– Helene, Elspeth says. My stepdaughter-in-law, she explains. Isabelle, an artist. And Alphonse.

– Come right in, the beauty says, her voice surprisingly husky.

– What's the matter with your voice? Elspeth asks her.

– It's that cold, Helene says. I still haven't got over it.

A balding middle-aged man, shiny, in pin-striped suit and pink-striped shirt, appears on the landing above them.

– Elspeth, Helene calls up to him. And her friends.

He comes down the stairs, his arms opening gradually as he approaches them.

He embraces Elspeth. – Elspeth, he says.

– Isabelle, an artist, Elspeth says. And Alphonse. Giles, my stepson.

He extends a soft hand, smelling of soap. – How do you do, Isabelle. How do you do, Alphonse.

– I'll make some coffee, Helene says.

Giles leads them into the drawing room, filled with books, pictures, bibelots, china shepherdesses and a baby grand piano, very black and gleaming.

Natasha goes to the French window and stands looking down into the small tree-filled garden.

– David is joining us, Giles says to his stepmother.

– David?

– Didn't he tell you?

– He's coming here? Now?

– Didn't he tell you?

– He never tells me anything, Elspeth says.

– He's coming on his own steam. He was in this part of town anyway.

– How extraordinary, Elspeth says. I don't see him at breakfast. I don't see him at lunch. I don't see him at dinner. I don't see him at home at all, in fact, and then I come to someone else's house for a visit and learn he's due.

– Hardly someone else's house, Giles says, smiling.

– Don't quibble, she says.

Helene comes in with the coffee and cakes on a silver tray.

– When did he tell you he was coming? Elspeth asks her stepson.

– When did David ring, darling? Giles asks his wife.

– And sugar? Helene says to Natasha.

– Everything, Natasha says at the window. I was looking at that cat in the tree, she adds.

– He belongs to the neighbours, Helene says. He has a nasty habit of dropping onto your shoulders out of the tree when you least expect it.

– Hey! Natasha says.

– Have two, Helene says, as Natasha takes a petit four.

– Is she getting deafer? Elspeth asks her stepson.

– A little, he says, moving away.

– Who is it who's coming? Alphonse asks, stepping up to Elspeth.

– The Baron.

– The Baron?

– He only wants to have a look at you, Elspeth says. He's jealous of my friends.

– I can't stay, Alphonse says. I really can't.

– Don't be silly, Elspeth says. We've only just arrived. Besides, it was your idea to come. You know I was against it.

– This is most awkward, Alphonse says. It really is.

– He can be quite charming when he wants, Elspeth says.

– Don't you realise where that puts me? Alphonse says.

– How do you take your coffee? Helene asks Alphonse.

– Black, please.

– Giles, Elspeth says, what we'd really like to do is have a quick look at the picture. I know Alphonse has other things to do.

– Which one?

– Why the Braque of course, Elspeth says. I've seen the others.

– But your friends haven't, Giles says, smiling at Natasha, who has left the window and joined them.

– The Braque, Alphonse says.

– And you? Giles says to Natasha.

– I'd like to see everything, Natasha says.

– Really? Giles says, looking into her large blue eyes.

– We can start with the Braque, Elspeth says. Alphonse may have to go.

– Yes, really, Natasha says, staring straight back at him and hugging her pink scarf to her.

– Come, Elspeth says, putting down her cup. I can't wait to see it.

They troop after Giles to the study. The curtains are drawn and they huddle at the door, staring into the darkness. Giles fiddles with the switches and the room gradually fills with light. A spotlight picks out a large canvas behind the desk.

– It was the middle of the war, Giles says, moving towards it. Everyone in Paris was starving. Artists paint what is closest to their hearts. Bread and ham were what was closest to Braque's heart at the time, and he painted that.

They stand in front of the desk and look.

– What do you think of it? Giles asks Natasha, who is standing next to him, hugging her pink scarf to her.

– I've only just begun to look, she says.

– I find, Giles says, that it is an enormously peaceful picture.

Alphonse, having strolled round the room examining the objects on display, is now standing at the window, lifting the edge of the curtain and looking out.

– Don't you? Giles says to Natasha.

– I don't know, Natasha says. I've only just begun to look.

Elspeth joins Alphonse at the window. – Well? she says.

– Charming, Alphonse says. Quite charming. But I wonder if perhaps we should be thinking of departing?

– There's plenty of time, Elspeth says.

– I have seen all I want to see, Alphonse says.

– Would you like to have a look at some of my other pictures? Giles asks Natasha.

– I haven't finished looking at this one.

– Of course.

Alphonse takes out a penknife and, opening it, slides the blade between the window and the frame.

– What are you doing? Elspeth says to him. Put that away! What on earth do you think you are doing?

– Calm yourself, Elspeth, Alphonse says, closing the knife and returning it to his pocket. Calm yourself please.

– I can't look with you standing there beside me like that, Natasha says to Giles. You put me off.

– I'll move away.

– No, no. I'll come back later. Show me your other pics.

– Does Beuys interest you? he asks as they make their way up the stairs. Does Polke?

There is a ring at the doorbell and movement in the hall, the sound of a door opening and voices raised in greeting.

– That will be the Baron, Elspeth says to Alphonse. Let us go out and greet him.

– In a minute, Alphonse says. I would like to have another look at the picture, I really would. He grabs her arm. Remember, he says, you do not know that I am acquainted with him.

– I'm looking forward to seeing his face, she says.

– I have some early Richters, Giles says as he ushers Natasha into his upstairs study. And one or two Kounellis.

– Show me where the loo is first, Natasha says.

Downstairs the Baron is in the hall, taking off his coat when his wife emerges from the study.

– Well, well, he says. What a pleasant surprise.

– We came to look at the Braque, Elspeth says.

– We?

– I've brought some friends along.

– So Giles said. Do I know them?

– I don't think so.

– And where are they? the Baron asks.

– One of them is still looking at the Braque. His friend is upstairs with Giles, looking at his collection.

Alphonse stands at the study door. The Baron stares at him. Alphonse advances doggedly, hand outstretched. – Alphonse, he says.

– Alphonse what?

– Just Alphonse.

– So pleased to meet you, the Baron says, ignoring the hand.

– Alphonse used to be a clown, Elspeth says.

– Really? the Baron says. A clown?

– An honourable profession, Alphonse says.

– No doubt, the Baron says. No doubt. And now?

– Banjo, Elspeth says. His clown name was Banjo.

– Banjo? Not Alphonse?

They move into the living room.

– All clowns have to have a name, Elspeth says. A clown name. For the posters. The children.

– And now? the Baron says. You do what?

– This and that, Alphonse says.

– Ah, the Baron says. I see.

| 52 |

– You know how it is, Alphonse says.

– Indeed I do, the Baron says. Indeed I do.

Giles returns, ushering in the tall Natasha, resplendent in her pink scarf.

– Isabelle, Elspeth says. Allow me to introduce my husband.

– Isabelle, the Baron says. A lovely name.

Natasha stands smiling at them, hugging her pink scarf to her.

– Come and sit beside me, the Baron says, making room for her on the sofa where he has seated himself.

– Isabelle is a painter, Elspeth says. And a sculptor. She makes things out of papier maché. Cars and things.

– Really? the Baron says. How interesting.

– Why is it interesting? Natasha asks, sitting down beside him.

– It's what one says, my dear, the Baron says.

– Don't my dear me, Natasha says.

– I'm sorry, he says.

– I hate that.

– You know, he says, there's something familiar about your voice.

– Perhaps you heard it in a dream, she says,

– Yes, the Baron says, staring at her. Perhaps I did.

– What have you done to this room? Elspeth asks her step-daughter-in-law.

– We had it redecorated.

– I can see that. But why this peculiar shade of green?

– We felt it would suit the room, Helene says.

– Did you?

– Yes, Helene says. I think it's rather successful.

— Do you?

— What exactly did she mean? the Baron asks Natasha. Papier maché cars?

— I haven't a clue, Natasha says.

— But you *are* a sculptor?

— I'm an art student.

— But you think of yourself as a sculptor?

— I paint, she says.

— How interesting.

— It's bloody boring most of the time.

— Why do you do it then?

— I don't know.

— How curious, the Baron says.

— It's the only thing I'm good at, I suppose, Natasha says.

— I'm sure that's not true.

— I dance well.

— So do I, the Baron says. Though I haven't danced for ages.

— My husband, Elspeth says, coming and standing over them, sometimes forgets his age.

— Age has nothing to do with it, the Baron says. He smiles at Natasha, pushing the mop of white curls off his forehead.

— You grew up in Hungary, I gather, Giles says to Alphonse.

— A painful time, Alphonse says. I prefer not to talk about it.

— Why painful?

— The war . . ., Alphonse says.

— Of course, Giles says.

— That's why I became a clown.

— Really? Giles says.

— I wanted to forget the past, Alphonse says. I wanted to put on a new face and make children laugh.

– You know what we should do, the Baron says to Natasha as Elspeth moves away. We should go dancing one of these days.

– Any time, Natasha says.

– Do you mean that?

– Of course.

– How do I get hold of you?

– Are you asking for my phone number?

– I suppose I am, the Baron says.

– I'll have to look it up, Natasha says. I've moved recently.

– Where have you moved to? the Baron asks, getting out his notebook and little gold pencil.

– Kennington.

– A charming borough.

– Bloody depressing, Natasha says.

– It isn't perhaps the most salubrious of neighbourhoods, the Baron says. But full of life.

– Why do you speak in that funny way? she asks, looking straight at him.

– Do I?

– Yes, she says. It sounds funny to me anyway.

– Perhaps it's because I'm nervous.

– Are you always nervous?

– No, he says, smiling and shaking his curls. You seem to bring it on.

She laughs.

Elspeth, who has been standing at the window, turns and says: We have to go.

– So soon?

– I dragged Alphonse and Isabelle away from their work, she says. I must return them to it.

[55]

The Baron writes down in his notebook the number Natasha reads out to him. — I'll call you and arrange a date, he says.

Alphonse shakes hands all round. — Goodbye, he says. Goodbye, goodbye, goodbye. And thank you so much for the opportunity to look at your lovely picture, he says to Giles.

— That's what pictures are for, Giles says. They are there to be looked at.

— Oh they are, Alphonse says. I agree with that. They really are.

Giles escorts them to the door. — If you want to have another look at the Braque, he says to Natasha, you know you're always welcome. Here's my card.

— Thanks, Natasha says. I'll take you up on that.

13

– Alphonse?

– Speaking.

– Thank God I've got you at last, Alphonse. What's going on?

– Is that the Baron?

– Of course it's the Baron. I want to know what's going on, Alphonse.

– Going on, Baron?

– Stop playing the fool, Alphonse. You know very well what I mean.

– You mean concerning this morning, Baron?

– To have you introduced as a friend of my wife's, Alphonse, it was most disconcerting.

– I think, Alphonse says, that I should be allowed to conduct my inquiry in my own way.

– I'm paying you, Alphonse. I think I have the right to know what you're up to.

– For reasons I will not go into, Alphonse says, it has proved necessary to befriend the lady. I –

– Alphonse, the Baron says, that is totally unacceptable. And what's more, you know it.

– I think you will have to let me be the judge of that, Baron, Alphonse says.

– But what are you up to, Alphonse? I mean it was a bit of a shock coming upon you like that at my son's.

– I'm afraid there was no time to warn you, Baron. I myself of course had no idea that you would be dropping in when I accepted the lady's invitation.

– But what were you doing accepting her invitation, Alphonse? How did you get to know her? And how long were you going to keep this from me?

– Baron, Baron, Alphonse says. Getting into a temper will help no one.

– She speaks of you as a friend, the Baron says. How long have you known her? And why didn't you report any of this to me?

– It's always best to keep it simple, Baron. It really is.

– Meaning what, Alphonse?

– Meaning that when I have the information relevant to our inquiry I will of course inform you. Until that time I think . . .

– What do you think, Alphonse?

– It's always best to keep it simple, Baron.

– And it's keeping it simple to befriend the subject of your inquiry? It's keeping it simple to gain access to my son's house and –

– Baron, Baron, Alphonse says, if you go on in this vein it will be impossible to do business with you, it really will.

– I want information, Alphonse, not silly games.

– You shall have it, Baron, Alphonse says. You really will. As soon as something emerges you will have it. In the meantime, I beg you to be patient.

– That woman's at the end of her tether, the Baron says. I need to know what she intends to do.

– I would say, Baron, that she is unlikely to do anything rash.

– You'd say that, Alphonse?

– I would, Baron.

– After a mere week or two's acquaintance?

– Baron, Alphonse says, this is my professional sphere. Please don't forget that.

There is a silence. Then the Baron says: Very well then, Alphonse. But there is a limit to my patience.

– Of course there is, Baron. Of course there is. As soon as the picture is clear you will be informed.

– And what does it mean, as soon as the picture is clear?

– It means, Baron, that as soon as I have the concrete information you asked for I will pass it on to you. Believe me, Baron, I am as keen to clear up the situation as you are, I really am.

– Is there another man, Alphonse? If so, what is she planning with him? If not, what's all this in her diary about? On the other hand, if –

– As soon as the picture is clear, Baron, Alphonse says. As soon as the picture is clear.

– And when will that be?

– Baron, Baron, Alphonse says. Do we have to go into all that again? When I have something precise to impart, Baron, I will. I cannot be clearer than that, Baron, I really can't.

– Very well then, the Baron says. Good day, Alphonse.

– And a very good day to you, Baron.

14

Felix is enjoying his meal. That is one advantage of being friends with the owner of a good restaurant, you can always count on a pleasurable meal.

– It's in the study, he says. On the left of the entrance hall, before the stairs. And it's big.

He tastes the risotto. – Excellent, he says.

– I have the best chef in town, Lino says. How big? he asks.

– From the way they talked, big.

– What's big?

– You better see it then, Lino. All I know is what I hear. It's a picture of some slices of bread and ham. He painted it when he was starving in Paris in 1943. He could think of nothing but food so he painted it.

– Maybe I should have it in here, Lino says.

– Who wants a picture when they can have the real thing? Felix says, cleaning his plate with a slice of bread. He puts the bread in his mouth and wipes his mouth with his napkin as he chews and swallows.

– I'll have to think about it, Lino says. Would you like a main course? I have some very nice osso bucco.

– No, no, Felix says. Just coffee.

– A nice dish of vitello tonnato?

– No, no. Just coffee.

– We have a very nice tiramisu tonight.

– Coffee will do me, Felix says. You know I'm not a great eater, Lino.

– Four million, Felix says, when Lino has placed the cup in front of him. Just for a piece of bread and some slices of ham.

– Maybe I should start charging more, Lino says, and laughs.

Felix stands up and takes his coat from the hanger. – That was a good meal, he says.

– I wish you'd tried the vitello tonnato.

– I'm sure it was excellent.

– I have the best chef in town, Lino says.

He accompanies Felix to the door. – Drop by, he says. Any time. It's always a pleasure to see you.

– And you, Felix says.

He hurries out into the drizzle.

15

Natasha walks into the café in the King's Road and sits down at Charlie's table. – It's got to stop, she says.

– What are you talking about?

– You know what I'm talking about, she says. I can't move without seeing you and your bloody camera. If I come out of the house you're standing on the other side of the square. If I'm in a shop you're filming me through the window. If I go into a supermarket you're in the next aisle. It's got to stop, Charlie.

– You're hallucinating, he says.

– I know I am, she says. But there's no smoke without a fire. I've seen you slipping into alleys when I turn round in the street. I've seen you getting off buses I've been on. I've seen you waiting outside the cinema when I've come out. I've seen you –

– You're nuts, he says.

– It's got to stop, she says. Or I'm quitting.

– You've quit anyway, he says. You're shacking up with this guy.

– Wanna bet?

– Aren't you?

– It's none of your business.

– It was, once.

– Never, she says.

– What's it mean, he says, you're quitting?

– I've looked for it everywhere, she says. I just can't find it. He's beginning to get suspicious.

– He's probably put it in the bank by now.

– Not him, she says. I know him.

– Why don't you admit you're sleeping with him? he says. I wouldn't mind. I'd be glad. I'd feel you'd got what you deserved.

– Shit, she says.

– Well, aren't you?

– I don't want to talk about it, she says. I told you. I said I'd do the job and I will. Now shut the fuck up.

– OK, OK, he says. But try to get a move on, will you?

– I want to get this straight first, she says. No more following me. No more cameras. Nothing.

– What are you talking about? he says.

– You think I haven't seen you? she says. With your camera? Snooping?

– You're crazy, he says.

– Why did you follow me the first day?

– I was worried about you.

– It was your idea.

– I know. But I was worried about you.

– You see, she says. I'm all in one piece.

– I know, he says. I should have known better.

– No snooping, she says. No camera. Nothing. Or the deal's off.

– We made a deal? he says. It's so long ago I've forgotten.

– It was your idea, she says. We made a deal. And I intend to keep my side of it. Just don't fuck it up.

– You're only doing it because it tickles your taste for adventure.

– Of course, she says. So what?

– Nothing, he says. Nothing.

– Don't tell me you're only doing it for the paper, she says.

– No, he admits. I enjoyed the scam.

– Remember, she says. No more camera. No more spying. Nothing. Or I swear the deal's off.

– OK, he says. But try to get a move on, will you.

16

– Miss Jenkin was in her usual excellent form, the Baron says as they leave the busy streets of Henley behind them.

– I'm very glad to hear it sir, Felix says.

– Her hearing is deteriorating, though, the Baron says. I asked her if everything was all right and she said, Oh, yes, beautifully. Beautifully? I said. He sings, she said. Sings? I said. In the middle of the night, she said. The night? I said. Night, she said. He sings in the middle of the night? I said. What are you talking about? she said. Who sings? I don't know, I said, I'm just repeating what you said. You're just trying to muddle me, she said. Do you think, Felix, the Baron asks, that it's her mind or her hearing that's going?

– I wouldn't venture to say, sir, Felix says.

With a sigh the Baron settles back into his seat. Only much later, as they are crossing over the M25, does he speak again.

– Felix, he says, this man you recommended to my friend. He has his own way of doing things, does he not?

– I think I suggested as much, sir, Felix says.

– He does not behave as my friend would have expected such a person to behave.

– I'm sorry to hear it, sir. I believe, though, that he has always given satisfaction, sir.

– That's what I wanted to ask you about, the Baron says. My friend has the feeling that he is not only idiosyncratic, he may also be incompetent.

— I'm sorry to hear that, sir, Felix says.

— You're sure he's up to scratch, are you, Felix?

Felix gives the car its head as they cruise up the motorway. With barely a sound they sweep past the rest of the traffic in the outside lane.

— Are you quite sure, Felix?

— I have always endeavoured to give satisfaction, sir, Felix says.

— Indeed, Felix, you have, the Baron says. But you have not answered my question.

— No, sir, Felix says, his eyes firmly on the road.

The Baron sighs. — I suppose you know best, Felix, he says.

— Thank you, sir, Felix says.

The Baron sighs again. He looks at his watch. — Sports report, Felix, he says, and as Felix fiddles with the knobs he settles back in his seat and closes his eyes.

On arrival Felix glances at the Baron and sees he is asleep. He coughs gently and the Baron opens his eyes. — Thank you, Felix, he says, unfastening his seat belt.

— If you will permit me, sir, Felix says, his handkerchief at the ready.

The Baron holds his face towards him, shaking the white curls off his forehead. — Thank you, Felix, he says again, as Felix gently wipes off the offending mark.

Felix returns the handkerchief to his pocket and, getting out of the car, hurries round to open the door for the Baron.

— That will be all for today, Felix, the Baron says as he gets out.

— Very good, sir, Felix says.

17

– Giles Baron speaking.

– This is Isabelle.

– Isabelle! How nice to hear from you.

– Listen. I'd love to come round and have another look at that Braque.

– Really? When would you like to come?

– When do you suggest?

– Tomorrow?

– That might be difficult. What about the day after?

– That's fine. About eleven, shall we say?

– No probs, Natasha says.

– I'll see you then, Giles says. I look forward to it.

– Me too, Natasha says.

•

– Hullo.

– Is that Isabelle?

– Speaking.

– It's the Baron here.

– Hullo!

– Isabelle, are you living with Alphonse?

– I have a room in his flat. Why?

– I've just realised. The number you gave me. It's the same as his.

– That's right.

– And that would explain why your voice seemed familiar when we met. We've talked on the phone before, haven't
we?

– Yes, she says.

– Is Alphonse there, Isabelle?

– No, I'm afraid not.

– Good. It's you I wanted to talk to.

– Yes?

– Isabelle, I was wondering if you'd like to come to dinner
with me here tonight?

– Here?

– In Highgate.

– I'd love to. What time.

– Shall we say around seven?

– You'll have to give me your address.

– Of course. Have you got pencil and paper to hand?

– Shoot.

•

– Lino? This is Charlie. Is Rosie there?

– Charlie! How are you, my dear? When will we see you,
Charlie?

– One of these days, Lino. One of these days.

– We have to talk business, OK?

– OK, Lino. I haven't forgotten.

– Wait. I pass you Rosie.

– Hi.

– Hi. You want to come out this evening?

– Sure.

– I'll see you in the café in half an hour.

– Can't you come round here?

[68]

– I don't want to see Lino.

– Oh, Charlie!

– He wants to talk business with me. I don't want to see him.

– OK. I'll see you at the café.

– Half an hour.

– Half an hour.

18

Elspeth is taking Alphonse out to lunch at one of her favourite restaurants, the Shalimar in Old Street.

– Alphonse, she says, I'm so worried. I don't know what's happening.

– Everything's taken care of, Alphonse says. It really is, Elspeth.

– That's what you always say, she says.

– And why do I say it? he says. Because it's true, Elspeth, it really is.

– You've taken my money, Alphonse, she says, and you've eaten my lunches, but you haven't done anything, nothing at all.

The waiter stands at their table. – I'll have the special, Vijay, she says.

– And for the gentleman?

– The same, Alphonse says. And a bottle of mineral water.

– No, she says. No mineral water. A jug of tap water for both of us, she says to the waiter.

– What do you mean, Elspeth? Alphonse says.

– You have twenty-eight more chances of being affected by radiation if you drink mineral water than if you drink tap water. It's common knowledge.

– Common knowledge? He says. What are you talking about, Elspeth?

– It stands to reason, she says. Radiation seeps down into

the earth and infects the springs of mineral water, deep inside the mountains.

– What radiation, Elspeth? he says.

– Radiation from Chernobyl, she says. And all the other bombs they've set off.

– And what about pollution? he says. What about the well-documented pollution of London tap water?

– Would you rather be polluted or radiated? she says. A jug of tap water, Vijay. With ice.

– You've taken my money, Alphonse, she says when the waiter has left, and you've eaten my lunches, but you haven't done anything, nothing at all.

– You said that already, he says. But how do you know? How do you know I haven't done anything?

– Nothing I paid you for, she says.

– Pay, pay, he says. There's the security angle to consider as well, you know.

– Of course I know, she says, lighting a new cigarette from the butt of the old one and stubbing out the butt in the ashtray. I'm not sure we should be eating together in public like this, Alphonse, but I had to talk to you.

– Slowly, bit by bit, Alphonse says, the pieces are starting to fall into place. Soon I will act and it will all be over.

– I don't want to know, she says. I want it done and that's all. I'm sick and tired of nothing happening, Alphonse, sick and tired, sick and tired.

– If you think it's easy why don't you do it yourself? he says.

She stares at him across the table, open-mouthed.

– You've no conception, Elspeth, he says, of the amount of planning that is required in an operation like this.

– You're not frightened, are you, Alphonse? she asks suddenly.

– Me? he says.

– You're not going to chicken out, are you? Take my money and run?

– Elspeth, he says, what is this chickening-out? Do I look as if I'm running?

– Just for a moment, she says, I thought that –

– Fear, Alphonse says, is not a word I understand.

The waiter brings the jug of iced water.

– Alphonse, she says, if something does not happen within the next week our arrangement is off and I will want my money back.

– Money, money, he says. Is that all you can think about, Elspeth? These things take time, they really do.

– This is all about my money, she says. I was poor once and I never intend to be poor again. If that baby is born, Alphonse, I'm written out of his will and then I won't even have enough money to pay you.

– Don't talk to me about poor, Elspeth, he says. When my father was –

– Alphonse, she says, this is my ultimatum: either you act by the end of next week or our arrangement is off and you return your advance.

– How can you say that, Elspeth? he says.

– I've just said it, haven't I? she says. And do sit up, Alphonse, I can't bear to see people lolling about in their chairs.

– If you want to shake hands and say goodbye, Alphonse says, then it's your affair. But a deal is a deal. What you paid me you paid me.

– You won't return it?

– No, Alphonse says.

– Then I'll have to find another way of getting it back, she says.

– Are you threatening me, Elspeth? he says. Is this what it has come to?

– I'm so frightened, Alphonse, she says. I don't know why you had to make me take you there. And now the Baron's found out we're friends who knows what he's going to do.

– I explained to you, Elspeth, Alphonse says. I had to see the lie of the land. Now I have seen it my plans have matured. They really have.

– What do you mean, *matured*, Alphonse?

– And as for the Baron, he says, I have explained to him that it was necessary to make your acquaintance in order to tail you more effectively.

– Don't say that word, Alphonse, she says.

– What word?

– I told you, she says. It makes me think of topped and tailed.

– You're too sensitive, Elspeth, he says.

– I don't like the associations, Alphonse.

– The Baron, he says, was surprised but he has wisely decided to let me get on with things in my own way.

– That's what I want to do too, she says. But you don't do anything. Your way is not to do anything. That's not what I paid you for, Alphonse.

– Elspeth, he says, I will be seriously angry if you go on talking like that. I really will. You pay me so that I can take the decisions, so why not leave me to make them?

– But that's just it, she says. You don't seem to take any

decisions. All you do is to take my money and eat my meals.

– Elspeth, he says, you are tired and overwrought. You really are. Leave it to me and I promise you will be paying me the rest of the money very soon.

– I can't stand the strain, Alphonse, she says. You've got to understand that.

– You shouldn't smoke so much, Elspeth, he says. You really shouldn't.

19

– That, says the Baron, is my wife's hammock. She likes to lie here in the afternoons and let the breeze rock her to sleep.

– Does she sleep a lot? Natasha asks.

– Unhappy people always sleep a lot, the Baron says.

– Why is she unhappy?

The Baron shrugs, looking at her from under his crop of white curls. – There are so many reasons to be unhappy in this life, he says.

– Yeah yeah, Natasha says.

They are in the garden, big as a football field, of the Baron's house in Highgate, on a fine spring evening. – Over there, the Baron says, is the cottage where Felix lives. Next to it is the greenhouse, and beyond that is the cottage where Wally the gardener and his family live.

– And that?

– What?

– Over there.

– Oh, he says. Hampstead Heath.

She whistles. – You've got yourself a nice set-up here, haven't you? she says.

– I'm very fond of it, the Baron says.

– How come you didn't buy Buckingham Palace?

– Oh, I much prefer Highgate to Victoria, don't you?

– Hey, Natasha says. I'm cold.

– The evenings are still quite chilly, the Baron agrees. Let's go inside.

He leads her into the house.

– This is a bit of a let-down, she says, surveying the living room.

– What is?

– All this, she says, waving vaguely.

– You think so?

– There's too much furniture in it.

– How extraordinary, he says. I have only ever been complimented on my furniture.

– Perhaps it's because I'm a big girl, she says. I'm always afraid of falling over things or knocking things down.

– You're not that big, he says.

– Compared to you I am, she says. But then you're practically a dwarf.

– Hold on, Isabelle, he says. Hold on.

– Well you are, she says.

– I think I'm pretty average, he says. Tall for a Welshman, as Dylan Thomas would say.

– Perhaps you are, she says. I'm sorry if I've offended you.

– Not at all, he says, motioning her to a sofa. I like your outspokenness. Now what will you have to drink?

– Campari, she says. And soda.

The Baron rings and Felix appears. – A Campari and soda for the lady, please, Felix, the Baron says.

– Very good, sir.

– You're not drinking? she asks as Felix disappears.

– Felix knows what I drink.

– OK, OK, she says. You needn't put me down.

– My dear girl, he says.

– I told you not to dear girl me, she says.

– Oh dear, he says.

She looks round.– Who's that? she asks.

– My late mother.

– And that's your father?

– My grandfather.

– And that?

– You *are* inquisitive, he says.

Felix brings in the drinks.

– If you've got them all over the walls I'd have thought you wouldn't mind saying who they were, she says.

– That's my daughter.

– Really? She doesn't look like either of you.

– Either of us? Oh, I see. She's not Elspeth's daughter. She does in fact resemble her mother.

– How many have you had?

– Children?

– No, wives.

– My, he says, you are curious.

She sips her drink and smiles at him over the rim of her glass. He smiles back at her, pushing the curls off his forehead.

– What shall we talk about then? she asks.

– My dear, he says. What a question to ask.

– Well, she says, everything I ask seems to be either out of bounds or I put my foot in it.

– You *are* direct, he says.

– What's the point of being indirect?

– I remember, he says, when I was a student at Oxford, I was invited to tea by a very famous and eccentric Russian professor. There must have been six or seven people there, besides the professor and his wife. We sat round a large circular table and he said: If this was an English tea party we would talk about the weather. But it is not an English tea party. It is a Russian tea party. So I suggest our topic of conversation today. I suggest we talk about the Devil.

– Why are you telling me this? she asks.

– I don't know, he says. I thought it might amuse you. It came to mind when you asked what the point of being indirect was.

– Go on, then, she says.

– Not if it bores you.

– Oh go on, she says. Now you've started. Did you talk about the Devil?

– I think so, he says. I don't remember much about that. Only his opening remarks and the size of the table. It was a very big round table. Beautifully polished. And with an inlay of darker wood round the circumference, a few inches in from the edge.

She is silent, finishing her drink.

– He lectured on Dostoevsky, he says. I went along, though I wasn't reading Russian. He lectured in English, with a strong Russian accent. It was some sort of graduate lecture because there weren't all that many of us. His wife sat at the back and barracked him. When he said, 'And then he married his secretary', she shouted: 'What secretary? She was the companion of his life, the reason for his success.' When he said: 'The portrait of Nastasya Filipovna is highly idealised, of course, but it is still remarkable', she cried out: 'Dostoevsky knew nothing about women, nothing!' We waited for these interjections because, though the lectures were fairly interesting, they were a little too religiose for our liking. And, besides, we were always hoping for an open fight between them.

– Who was Nastasya Filipovna? she asks.

Felix stands at the door. – Dinner is served, sir, he says.

The Baron takes her arm and guides her into the circular tapestried dining room. He pulls a tall-backed chair out for her and helps her to settle before assuming his own place opposite her. When they are settled Felix approaches, holding a silver dish in white gloves, and bends over her.

– Hey! she says. Do I have to?

– Felix can help you if you prefer.

– No, no. I'll manage. But I'll probably send it all over the tablecloth.

– A simple soufflé, the Baron says. I hope you will find it to your liking.

– Does he serve you when you eat here alone? she asks when Felix has gone.

– Occasionally, the Baron says, his eyes twinkling.

– I couldn't bear it, she says.

– It all depends on what you're used to, he says.

– Did you grow up with this, then?

– No, oh no, he says. Though I did not grow up *poor*. I had a certain *start* in life.

She tucks into her soufflé, wipes her mouth with the big starched napkin, looks at him. – Are you happy? she asks.

– The questions you ask! he says.

– Well, are you?

– Most of the time, he says. I would say I had a sunny disposition.

– Why do you speak like that? she says.

– Like what?

– I don't know. The way you speak. The words you use.

– I told you, he says. It's your presence that brings it on. You make me nervous.

She laughs.

– Why do you laugh?

– Because you feel nervous with me and I feel so relaxed with you. It should be the other way round, shouldn't it?

– I'm glad you feel relaxed, he says.

She is silent, her brow furrowed.

– And you? he asks.

– Me?

– Are you happy?

– Oh no, she says. How could I be, at my age?

– I thought the young were happy. Without a care in the world.

– Then you've forgotten what it's like to be young, she says.

Felix comes round with the soufflé for the second time. – I don't know, she says. Is there a lot to follow?

– A fair amount, he says, smiling at her.

– Then perhaps I shouldn't have any more.

– Go on, he says. You're a growing girl.

– I hope not, she says. But I tell you what, I'm pretty happy this evening. And happiness is good for the digestion. So I won't hold back.

– I'm glad, he says.

•

After the meal he leads her back to the living room. – Will you have a liqueur? he asks.

– Yes please. A kirsch.

She lights a cigarette.

– I'd rather you didn't smoke, he says.

– I'll go outside.

– No, if you must, smoke here.

– But you said I shouldn't.

– I said I'd rather you didn't.

– Then I won't. It's not important.

Felix brings in the coffee. – A kirsch for the lady, the Baron says.

– Very good sir, Felix says.

Natasha looks at her watch. – I should go, she says.

– Because I asked you not to smoke?

– No. I just feel I should go.

– But you've only just arrived.

– You invited me to dinner.

– Dinner was just the first part of the evening, he says.

– And what do we do for the second part?

He laughs.

– I'm sorry, she says. I'm not used to sitting around. I'm used to doing things.

– Perhaps we could go dancing, he says.

– Not tonight.

– Another time?

– I told you I'd like that.

– Would you rather have gone dancing tonight?

– No. I'm glad I came. But I must go now.

She stands up.

– You're really set on going?

– Yes.

– And that kirsch?

– Another time.

– In that case I'll ask Felix to drive you.

[81]

– No, no. I can make my own way.

– It's no trouble.

– I'll make my own way.

– As you wish, he says.

– I really enjoyed it, she says.

– You're a funny woman, Isabelle, he says.

– Am I? Why do you say that?

– Has no one said it to you before?

– No, she says. My friends just take me as I am.

She bends a little and kisses him on the cheek. – Thank you for a wonderful dinner, she says.

– And that dance?

– Just ring me up.

– I wanted to ask you about Alphonse.

– It's not important, she says.

He escorts her to the door.

– Ring me, she says.

– Of course, he says, smiling at her and pushing the curls out of his eyes. Of course.

20

The sound of the accordion fills the stairwell as she climbs, and, behind it, Alphonse's mournful, slightly reedy voice. When she enters she finds him sitting in the big armchair, the accordion round his shoulders, a cushion on his lap, a bottle of wine between his legs.

– Where have you been, my poppet? he asks.

– Are your balls cold? she says, pointing to the cushion.

– I asked where you'd been.

She goes into the kitchen, takes a bottle of mineral water out of the fridge, picks up a glass and comes back into the room.

– I asked you a question, he says.

– Oh fuck off, she says. She fills the glass, drains it, fills it again.

He lifts the bottle of wine to his lips, drinks, puts the bottle down at his feet again, wipes his mouth, hoists the accordion on to his chest and begins to play again. As he plays he sings.

When he stops she says: What's that?

– It's a song the peasant women used to sing in my child-hood. It was written by our greatest poet, Petőfi.

– What does it say?

– It's in Hungarian.

– I asked what it said.

– A rough English translation would go like this, he says. He begins to sing again:

I'll be a tree if you are the tree's blossom
If dew you are, a flower I will become,
I'll be the dew if you're a beam of sunlight
So that our beings may be fused as one.

If it should be, sweet maiden, you are heaven,
I will at once be turned into a star.
If, sweetest maiden, you are hell itself,
I'll damn myself to join you where you are.

– I suppose it's better in Hungarian, she says, when it is clear he has finished.

He levers the accordion off his shoulders and lays it on the floor next to the bottle. – Petőfi was one of the leaders of the 1848 revolution, he says. He was probably killed at the age of twenty-six by the Tsar's army on the battlefield at Segesvar in 1849, though his body was never found.

– He wrote poetry like that?

– Isabelle, Alphonse says. Do you know what happens to me when I enter my room?

– When you enter your room?

– I stand in the middle of my room, Alphonse says, and I feel as if I am made out of glass. If someone were to look at me, Isabelle, he says, they would see right through me. If I were to knock on my chest with a spoon, Isabelle, he says, it would tinkle. Tinkle. And if I were to knock my leg against the bed it would shatter like glass. Have you ever felt like that, Isabelle? As if you were entirely made of glass?

– You're drunk, she says.

– When I feel like that, he says, only the poetry of Petőfi can save me. Only my accordion can save me. Do you know

[84]

what it means, Isabelle, to feel that only poetry can save you? That only the accordion can save you?

– You fucking lunatic, she says. You're blind drunk. You don't know what you're talking about.

– Isabelle, he says, someone has been going through my things. They really have.

– Someone?

– Going through my drawers.

– You've lost something?

– I don't like it, Isabelle.

– I asked if you'd lost something.

– I don't like people going through my drawers, he says.

– I should think not, she says.

He tosses the cushion onto the floor.

– What the fuck's that? she says.

– It's a gun, my poppet.

– You're going to shoot me?

– I might, my poppet, he says. I really might.

– You're drunk, she says. You're fucking drunk, Alphonse. Put that gun away before it goes off.

– It's silent, my poppet, he says. Silent as the grave. Almost.

– Put it away.

– You don't believe I'd shoot?

– Put it away, she says, you drunken sod.

There is a sound like a soda bottle being opened and the gun jerks in his hand.

– Fucking hell, she says. They look up at the ceiling, where the bullet has left a hole in the plaster.

– You let it off, you drunken lunatic, she says.

– You didn't think I would, did you, my poppet? he says, aiming the gun at her.

– Put it away, she says. You'll hurt somebody with that thing.

– Of course I will, he says. That's what it's for.

– Put that fucking gun away, she says, her eyes wide.

– Yes, my poppet, he says. He lays it down again on his knees. It's just so you can see what I can do, he says.

She stares at him.

– Only joking, he says.

– Fuck your jokes, she says.

21

– The essence of life, the Baron says, is flexibility. Do you not think so, Felix?

– Indeed, sir, Felix says, his eyes on the road.

– The trouble with Miss Jenkin, the Baron says, is her rigidity. Do you think rigidity is essential to those who seek to train the young, Felix?

– I wouldn't know, sir, Felix says.

– One sees the harm done to children by undue flexibility, of course, the Baron says.

– Children, the Baron says after a while, need to feel that there is some order in the world. They need something to rebel against. Is that not the essence of childhood, Felix?

– I cannot say, sir.

– Your own childhood was not happy, Felix?

– I have nothing to compare it with, sir, Felix says.

– That's very good, Felix, the Baron says. Very good. Did you make it up or did you read it somewhere?

– I beg your pardon, sir?

– No, that's quite all right, Felix, the Baron says. That's quite all right.

It is a while before the Baron speaks again. Then he says: That man you recommended to my friend, Felix, has proved something of a disappointment.

– I'm sorry to hear that, sir.

– Yes, Felix, it seems that he has been unable to find

anything. Nothing at all.

– Perhaps there was nothing to find, sir, Felix says, letting the big car run free on the outer lane of the motorway.

– There is always something to find, Felix, the Baron says. Believe me. Always.

– My friend is thinking of dispensing with his services, the Baron says after a while. He cannot continue to wait indefinitely.

– I am sorry to hear it, sir, Felix says.

– Do you think I should suggest he be patient for a little while longer, Felix?

– I would not like to say, sir.

– Of course, Felix, the Baron says. I quite understand.

He shifts in his seat to find a comfortable position. He looks at his watch. – Sports report, Felix, he says. Sports report. And later, when the classified results are being read out by James Alexander Gordon, as they have been every Saturday afternoon for as long as anyone can remember: Ah, Nottingham Forest. Do you remember their glory days, Felix? How are the mighty fallen! How are the mighty fallen!

When Felix eventually brings the car to a stop in the driveway of the big house in Highgate the Baron appears to be asleep. Felix coughs gently and the Baron opens his eyes. – Have we arrived, Felix? he asks.

– We have, sir.

– Very good, the Baron says, straightening up.

– If you will permit me, sir, Felix says, his handkerchief at the ready.

– Oh those girls! The Baron chuckles as Felix carefully wipes his cheek and chin. They'll be the death of me one of these days.

Felix returns the handkerchief to his breast pocket.

– Do you not think so, Felix? the Baron asks.

– Not with your constitution, sir, Felix says.

– You think so, Felix?

– I am sure of it, sir.

– Thank you, Felix, the Baron says. You reassure me.

22

Charlie is in the back of the restaurant, playing chess with Lino.

– Charlie, Lino says, how about you take some photographs of the restaurant? For publicity purposes.

– I don't do that sort of photography, Lino, Charlie says.

– But you can do it?

– No problem, Charlie says. But I don't.

– Not for me? Lino says.

Charlie moves a pawn forward.

– I pay, of course, Lino says.

– How much?

– Now you're talking, Lino says, taking the pawn with his bishop.

– How much?

– I will explain what I want, Lino says, and you name me a price.

Charlie looks at his watch. – I have to go, he says, pushing back his chair.

– Finish the game, Lino says. Finish the game. You have plenty of time.

– No, Charlie says.

He walks over to the coat stand, takes down his jacket. – I wanted to ask about your friend, he says, as he puts it on.

– What friend?

– Alphonse.

– You know him?

– He's a good friend?

– How come you know him?

– He's a good friend?

– More than a friend, Lino says. We're brothers.

– Brothers?

– Like brothers. From the old home.

– I thought he was Hungarian.

– Hungarian? Who told you that?

– I heard.

– No, no, Lino says. He's from my village. Who said he was Hungarian?

– He told Natasha.

– He knows Natasha?

– Yeah. He told her.

– He's a joker, Lino says. You mustn't believe everything he says. You take it with salt.

– A pinch of salt.

– Exactly. You take what he says like that.

– Why should he lie to her?

– Is not a lie, Lino says. Is a joke.

– I don't get the joke, Charlie says. Can you explain it to me?

– Just a joke, Lino says. Not a lie. No.

– And he was a clown? Is that true?

– Of course he was. Wonderful clown. You should have seen him. His name was Banjo.

– Banjo? Where does Alphonse come in, then?

– From my village. I told you.

– No. Where does his name come from?

– Is Alfonso, Lino says.

– Then why does he pronounce it the French way?

– He's a crazy man, Lino says. Big joker.

– I see, Charlie says.

– We'll talk on the phone, eh, Charlie? Lino says, accompanying him to the door. I tell you what I want and you name a price, OK?

– OK, Charlie says.

23

Giles, in his pin-stripe suit, opens the door and the welcoming smile freezes on his face.

– This is my friend Rosie, Natasha says. I hope you don't mind my bringing her along?

– I thought you'd be on your own, Giles says.

– Rosie's very interested in Beuys, Natasha says. I so much wanted her to see the drawings.

He stands in the doorway.

– Well? she says. Aren't you going to let us in?

– Of course, he says. Of course.

– Cheer up, she says as she brushes past him. It's not the end of the world.

– Tash was very enthusiastic about your collection, Rosie says as they stand in the large entrance hall.

– Tash? Giles says.

– They call me that, Natasha says.

– Why?

– God knows, she says.

– It's quite all right, he says to Rosie. Only I think you might have let me know, he says to Natasha in a whisper.

– Don't be so prissy, she says.

He leads them upstairs.

– You might have let me know, he says again to Natasha as Rosie examines the drawings.

– Oh stop it, she says, stepping up to join her friend.

– What do you think of them? Giles asks, coming round to her other side.

– Interesting, Rosie says.

– I'm hoping to acquire two more next week, he says. They are coming up for sale in Düsseldorf.

– Oh yes?

– It doesn't happen very often, he says.

– You're going yourself? Natasha asks him.

– Oh yes, he says. I always do. Would you like to come with me?

– We'll see, Natasha says.

– That one there, he says, I was very lucky with. It belonged to the estate of Count Fab –

– How about some coffee? Natasha says.

– Of course. But let your friend have a good look first.

– I'm dying for coffee, Natasha says.

– I'm almost finished, Rosie says.

– As I was saying, Giles says, it belonged to the estate of Count Fabrizio Fontanelli. In the eighties his widow –

There is a ring at the doorbell.

– Damn, Giles says. Excuse me, he says, and hurries out of the room.

They follow him down the stairs.

– Only the yellow pages, he says sadly, closing the door and looking up at them. I'm always hoping for mail, he says.

– Shall we have coffee? Natasha says.

– Have you finished looking?

– For the moment, thank you, Rosie says.

He opens the living-room door. – Make yourselves comfortable, he says. I'll bring it in a second.

– We could have it in the kitchen, Natasha says.

– No, no. Make yourselves comfortable here. I'll be with you in a jiffy.

– May we see the Braque? Rosie asks when they are finally settled with their coffee and biscuits.

– Braque interests you?

– Not as much as Beuys. But as I'm here . . .

– Of course, he says. Pictures, I always say, are there to be looked at. But let us have our coffee first.

– Where's Helene? Natasha asks.

– She's . . . away, he says.

– Pity, Natasha says.

He stands up. – Shall we see the Braque, then? he asks.

They follow him into the study.

•

Charlie, backing into the small front garden of the house on the opposite side of the road, pushes his video camera through a hole in the hedge and trains it on the front door.

– Excuse me.

Busy with his camera, he does not immediately realise he is being addressed.

– Excuse me.

He turns. A woman is leaning out of the ground-floor window, her hair blowing about her face. – Can I help you? she asks sweetly.

– No thanks, he says. I'm just focusing this.

– It's not a public thoroughfare, you know, she says.

He straightens. – Is this your house? he asks her.

– And garden, she says.

– Look, he says, do you mind if I settle here? I need to film that house across the street.

– Do you? she says. Why?

– I just do.

– Why?

– I'm an artist.

– Why that house?

– It appeals to me.

– You can't do it from here, she says. If you don't get out this instant I shall call the police.

– I'll let you see the film, he says, grinning at her.

– If you don't get out this instant I shall call the police, she repeats.

He sighs. Then, whistling, starts to pack away his camera.

– If you want to make use of people's private gardens, she says, you ask.

– Would you have let me if I had?

– No, she says.

She shuts the window with a bang, stares out at him through the pane, then disappears.

Whistling, Charlie walks down the road, then, looking round quickly, ducks into another garden.

24

– It shouldn't be difficult, Lino says to the man in Amsterdam. There's an alarm, of course, but that's all. In fact it wouldn't surprise me if they were after the insurance.

– You mean he wants it nicked?

– It wouldn't surprise me, Lino says.

– He'll make it easy for us?

– It wouldn't surprise me, Lino says again.

– I hope you're right.

– I'm right, Lino says. But it's big. It'll need a van.

– I'll get a van. What date are we talking about?

– I'll let you know, Lino says.

25

– It's Isabelle, Natasha says.

– Ah yes.

– Look, I'm sorry about the other day. She really did want to see those pictures.

– You might have warned me.

– May I come and see you on my own one of these days?

– What day did you have in mind?

– Not tonight, Natasha says. Otherwise I'm free.

– I'll have to call you back, he says. There are things to arrange.

– Arrange them, she says.

– I'll see what I can do, Giles says.

– I don't think I can go through with it, she says to Alphonse as she puts down the phone.

– Of course you can.

– He gives me the creeps.

– You don't have to do anything.

– You think so? she says. You think I don't have to do anything?

– Hold on, Isabelle, he says. What's the matter with you?

– You need your head examined, she says, if you think I don't have to do anything.

– I mean it, he says. I really do. With a man like that it's easy.

– You go then.

– He doesn't want me, he wants you.

– Maybe he's confused. Maybe it's you he wants.

– My dear Isabelle, he says.

– Don't dear Isabelle me, she says.

– But you will go, won't you?

– I'll see, she says.

– Just set him up this time, he says, and next time I come along with the camera and bingo.

– I'll see, she says again.

– What's the point of us working together if we don't work together?

– It was your idea, she says.

– Of course it was my idea. As soon as I saw you nick that wallet I knew we two could work together.

– I don't think it's such a good idea, she says.

– Isabelle, he says, I need you to do this one.

– I just don't think it's such a good idea. I have my career to consider.

– What's that? he says.

– My art, she says.

– This is your art, Isabelle, he says. Believe me. I have seen him look at you. I have seen the Baron look at you. This is your art.

26

– It's you again, she says.

– Hi! Charlie says.

– I thought I told you to keep out of my garden.

– Don't be like that, he says.

– Who are you anyway?

– My name's Charlie.

– Charlie, I want you to put away your camera and get out of my garden. I won't have you snooping about like that. Do you work for a paper?

– I told you, he says. I'm an artist.

– What does that mean?

– It means I work for myself. I'd love to film you, he says, smiling at her. I'd love to photograph you.

She strides up the steps to her front door, her shopping bags in her hands. – If you're not out of my garden in three minutes I'll call the police, she says.

– What have the police to do with it?

– They'll get you out of here.

– We need to talk, he says. Won't you let me photograph you?

She inserts the key in the lock, pushes open the door.

– Don't be like that, he says. I need to be in your garden for my project.

– What project is that?

– Do you want me to explain it to you?

– Go away, she says. Just go away. And don't come back. Understood?

·

– Just a few shots of the interior, Lino says. Tasteful. And one of the exterior. And then perhaps one or two of the staff. Vittorio. The chef. You know.

– I'm not a photographer, Lino, Charlie says.

– I pay well, Lino says. Your move.

– How well? Charlie says, staring at the board.

– You show me the photos and I pay you for them, Lino says.

– I'm expensive, Charlie says.

– If it's good I pay well.

– Can't you hire a professional?

– I like to keep it in the family.

– I'm not the family, Lino.

– You know what I mean, Lino says. Your move.

– You take whatever I give you? Charlie asks, moving his rook.

– You won't let me down, Lino says. I know that, Charlie. Rosie says you're the best.

– You believe what she says?

– I trust her judgement, Lino says. Check.

– I'll have to think about it, Charlie says.

– Don't think about it too long, Charlie, Lino says. I want to put them in my brochure.

– You've got me there, Charlie says.

– Yes, Lino says. This time I have.

– I'll do it for you, Charlie says. As a gesture of friendship.

– I know, Charlie, I know, Lino says, packing away the pieces. We're all friends here. And I'll pay what you ask.

27

– I tried to get the key in but it wouldn't turn, Helene says to her husband when he gets back.

– It was the wrong key.

– No it wasn't. I had to get in by the kitchen in the end. But now I've tried it again and it turns.

– You tried the wrong key, he says.

– I didn't, I tell you. And then there was someone in the garden.

– What are you talking about?

– I could have sworn there was someone. I knew as soon as I came round the side of the house. Behind the beech tree.

– You were dreaming, he says.

– I called to him to come out, she says, but he didn't. He didn't move.

– There you are, he says. You were imagining it.

– Come, she says.

– Come where?

– I want to show you something.

– Is this necessary? he asks as he follows her on to the small terrace at the back and then down the wrought-iron staircase into the little garden.

– You'll see, she says.

She marches to the end of the garden, round behind the big copper beech, points to the ground.

– A cigarette stub, he says. So what?

– Do you believe me now?

– Why believe you?

– There was someone here. Standing behind the tree.

– Smoking a cigarette?

– Well, why not?

– What, according to you, was he doing?

– How should I know? she says. He stopped me going in the front door so I'd come round by the back. Then he waited for me.

– But if he waited for you why didn't he make himself known to you?

– I don't know, she says. I don't know anything. She starts to cry.

– Willy could have thrown it over the wall, he says.

– He's given up.

– He might have started again.

– When did he ever throw anything over the wall?

– Well, a visitor then.

– It's been stubbed out.

– He stubbed it out and threw it over the wall.

– Try something else, Giles.

– The wind carried it.

– Can't you use your eyes? she says. It's been crushed into the grass.

He bends and looks. – Not necessarily, he says.

– What then?

– The wind could have carried it.

– I see, she says.

He turns back towards the house. She utters a scream.

– What is it? he cries, swinging round.

– Oh my God! she says, crouching under the tree, her hands over her shoulders.

– Helene! he says, hurrying back to her. What is it?

– That cat! she says. She starts to cry again.

– Look! she says, pointing. Look! On the wall!

– He fell on you?

– The bastard! she says. I could have miscarried. He should be shot. Shoo! Shoo!

The cat disappears over the wall.

– I wonder if he's taken up smoking, Giles says.

– You're unspeakable! She says. Unspeakable!

– Come, he says, helping her up. Come inside.

– Let me go! she says, wiping her eyes with her sleeve. Just let me go! Just let me go!

He follows her into the house.

28

Natasha and the Baron are having a little light refreshment at U Choose in Covent Garden after their exertions.

– I haven't felt so tired since I ran the London Marathon, the Baron says, his face crimson under his white curls.

– You? she says. You ran the London Marathon?

– What will you have to finish with?

– Strawberries please.

– Cream?

– Oh yes.

When he has ordered she says: I don't believe you about the London Marathon.

– It's true, he says. I was quite a runner in my time.

She opens her large blue eyes even wider. – Are you trying to impress me?

– I wouldn't dream of doing that, he says. He wiggles his arms. – I read the other day, he says, that doctors are advising us older folk to take it easy on the dance floor. You can rupture something, apparently.

– You can't rupture anything, she says. You're the fittest old man I've ever seen.

– Thanks, he says.

– I didn't mean that, she says. I'm sorry. I really enjoyed myself tonight.

The strawberries arrive. – I haven't been dancing for ages, she says. I really needed that.

– Why?

– Why what?

– Why haven't you been dancing?

– I quarrelled with my boyfriend.

– Alphonse?

– What Alphonse?

– I thought . . .

– Don't be ridiculous! she says.

– I thought . . .

– I have a room in his flat, that's all.

– That's all?

– What do you think?

– I don't really know what I think.

They eat their strawberries in silence.

– None of my wives has been the least bit interested in dancing, he says. Though Elspeth was what you might call a dancer when I met her.

– What does that mean?

– It means she trained at The Place in the Martha Graham tradition of modern dance.

– And then?

– Then what?

– Did she have a career?

– Not really, he says.

– Why not?

– You'll have to ask her, he says.

– You can't get too big, she says. Not with modern dance.

– You'll have to ask her, he says.

– These were good, she says.

– Have some more.

– May I?

– Of course.

– You dance well, she says, while they are waiting for the second helping of strawberries to arrive.

– You think so?

– Come on, she says. Don't fish for compliments.

– I'm not fishing, he says. I meant the question.

– I told you, she says.

– I was considered quite a good dancer once, he says. But that was a long time ago.

– You have that sort of body, she says.

– Dear Isabelle, he says. What a strange young woman you are.

– Why?

– I never know what you're going to say next.

– But one doesn't, does one? she says.

– You'd be surprised how predictable most people are. You're just the opposite.

– I am?

– You are. Now, he says. What will you have to follow? They do very good cakes here.

– I'm hungry as an ox, she says. Dancing always does that to me. I'm sorry.

– I like to see you eat, he says.

29

Coming down the aisle with her trolley full of food she suddenly finds a man there blocking her way.

– Hullo, he says.

– Do I know you?

– I'm the man in your garden.

– Oh, that one.

She tries to get the trolley past him.

– No, no, he says. Please.

– Please what?

– Don't hurry past. I'd like to invite you to coffee.

– Get out of my way, she says.

– Please, he says. I'd like to explain. Apologise.

– There's no need, she says.

– I'd like to photograph you, he says.

– Me? Why?

– Because you're beautiful.

– Oh come on, she says, trying to get past him again.

– I could take some lovely photos of you, he says.

– Look, she says, are you going to let me through or do I have to call an attendant?

He stands back as she pushes the trolley past him.

But he is waiting for her at the exit. – Let me carry your bags, he says.

– No, no, she says. I can manage.

– Please.

He takes one of her shopping bags. – I thought, he says, we could have a cup of coffee in here.

She follows him inside.

– I don't know why I'm doing this, she says as they sit down at a table in the corner.

– Politeness, he says. You don't want to hurt my feelings.

– That must be it, she says.

– My name's Charlie, he says, holding a hand out across the table.

– Mine's Karen.

– Hullo, Karen.

– What did you want to talk to me about?

– Not about, he says. I just wanted to talk to you. I wanted to try and persuade you to pose for me.

– What made you think I might?

– I didn't think. I'd like you to pose for me.

– You said you were an artist?

– Video artist. At present.

– What does that mean?

– One evolves.

– What are you doing with the house opposite?

– I'm doing this series about doors, he says.

– What about them?

– I'm interested in doors.

– Any particular aspect?

– I find them interesting.

– You must do, if you're doing a series about them. I want to know why.

– Think about it, he says.

The waiter brings their coffee.

– Why that one in particular?

– Why not? There are so many doors that one has to have a principle of selection. That one came up.

– What's the principle?

– Professional secret, he says. Sorry.

– How far are you with your series? she asks, opening a packet of sugar into her cup.

– I've done a restaurant. And a warehouse.

– How many will the series have?

– We'll see, he says. At first I tried to link it to my past. You know. The streets I've lived in. The houses I've lived in. But there wasn't enough variety and it was too personal anyway. So I opened up.

– You think a door's personal?

– You're very beautiful, Karen, he says. Will you let me photograph you?

– I might, she says.

– Say you will.

– I haven't made up my mind.

– I could fit in to your schedule, he says. My time's my own.

– You'd have to, she says. I have a very jealous husband and a very demanding daughter.

– What does she demand?

– Look, she says, can I ring you?

– Of course. Here's my card. I'll wait for your call. With impatience.

She gets up.

– No, she says as he pushes back his chair. I can manage. Thank you.

– I'll wait to hear from you, he says.

– Maybe, she says.

30

– You'll be on your own this time? Giles asks.

– Of course, Natasha says.

– Don't say of course like that, Giles says. You brought that friend of yours along last time when I thought you'd be on your own.

– Of course, Natasha says. She wanted to see your paintings.

– Don't keep saying of course, Giles says. I can't stand it.

– Hey! Natasha says. Cool it. Just cool it.

– What are you talking about? he says.

When she remains silent he says: It's not so easy making all the arrangements, you know.

– That's your prob, Natasha says.

– Of course it's my problem, he says. What's the matter with you?

– Just cool it, she says.

– Do you want to come or don't you? he says. It's entirely your decision.

– Of course it's my decision.

– Then are you coming?

– No, she says. Yes.

– Yes or no?

– Yes, she says.

– I'll ring you back, he says.

She puts down the phone. She says to Alphonse: I can't go through with it.

– Of course you can, my poppet, he says.

– Cut that out, she says.

– Sorry, he says. Only joking.

– I don't like your jokes.

– Isabelle, he says. You will do this thing because we have agreed on it. Is that understood?

– I'll see, she says.

– There's another thing, he says. I thought I told you to keep your hands off my things?

– What do you mean?

– I mean someone's been looking for something among my things. I don't like it, Isabelle. I really don't.

– Why should I go through your fucking things?

– If you didn't then who did?

– Search me, she says.

– You won't find anything, he says. There's nothing to find. With me what you see is what you get.

– Oh fuck off, she says.

– You see this? he says.

– Put it away, she says. Put it away.

– You think I don't know how to use it?

– I'm sure you know how to use it. You put a bullet through the ceiling the last time you used it.

– There's no chance of an accident when I'm holding it, he says. I'm warning you, Isabelle, for the last time. Don't fool with Alphonse.

– Sure, sure, she says. Now put it way.

He puts the gun back in the drawer, pockets the key. He grins at her. – You don't take me seriously, Isabelle, he says. But one day you will.

– Dream on, she says.

31

– Papa, Rosie says, Charlie and I want to get married.

– Married? Lino says. To that man?

– What's wrong with him?

– He's an artist.

– So? I'm an artist too, Papa.

– No, no, *cara*, you're an art student.

– So? What am I an art student for if I don't want to become an artist?

– It's different for a woman, Lino says.

– You're out of date by about a century, Papa, Rosie says. Anyway, we want to get married.

– Not on my life, he says.

– Why not, Papa?

– He's an artist is why, *cara*. He doesn't have a job.

– His job's being an artist, Papa.

– Let him show me his bank account, *cara*, Lino says. Until then I don't want to hear another word about this. Understand?

– Oh, Papa, she says.

– That's what happens when I let you go to art school, he says.

– But you like him, Papa. You like his work. You asked him to do some photos for you.

– He takes good pictures, Lino says. And he's cheaper than a professional.

– Successful artists make a lot more than you do, Papa, she says.

– How many are successful?

– Charlie's going to be successful.

– Good, he says. I'm very glad. When he's successful he can talk to me.

– No, Papa, we want to get married now.

– He can get married any time, Lino says. Who's stopping him?

– I said we, she says.

– *Cara*, he says, don't talk to me about this nonsense again. If he wants he can come and see me and bring his bank statements with him. But even then I can't promise anything. He's unreliable.

– He's beautiful, she says.

– Beautiful but unreliable.

– You'll be sorry, papa.

– Go away now, he says. You're making me angry.

– You'll be sorry, she says again.

32

— Are you going to take me on a tour of your house? Charlie asks.

— Why? Karen says.

— I love seeing the inside of other people's houses.

— I don't think so.

— You don't think I love seeing the inside of other people's houses?

— I don't think I'll give you a tour.

— Show me your study.

— Why?

— I want to see where you work.

— All right, she says.

She leads the way up the stairs, opens a door, stands back to let him pass.

— Very nice, he says.

He goes to the window.

— Very nice, he says again.

— What?

— The view.

— What view? she says.

— You writers, he says. You never use your eyes.

— I'm not a writer, she says. I'm a humble translator.

He remains at the window. — Come here, he says.

She joins him at the window.

— Stand there, he says. Look out.

– What are you doing?

– Just stand there. Keep looking out. Look down the street.

– Are you taking a picture of me?

– What do you think?

She turns and looks at him and he snaps her again.

– Why here? she says.

– It's your workroom, he says. You feel comfortable in it.

– Can we go down now?

– Of course.

– What are they for? she asks.

– Stop, he says to her on the stairs, and snaps her again as she turns to look up at him.

– What are they for? she asks again.

– I don't know, he says. I like shots of women in houses. A house is part of what we are.

– Sometimes, she says.

– What do you mean?

– I don't know, she says. Come on down and I'll make some coffee.

– Would you mind very much if I didn't have coffee?

– What would you like?

– I really ought to be going.

– Already?

– Yes, he says. But I'd like to come back. Now I'm getting to know the house. And you. I'd like to take some more.

– You're sure you want to go?

He smiles at her. – No, he says. But I have to. Really.

He kisses her on the cheek. – Can I phone you?

– In the mornings, she says. You can always get me in the mornings. After nine. Before eleven.

33

— Why, Natasha says to the Baron, are you hiring Alphonse to tail your wife?

— Really, Isabelle, he says.

— Why? she asks again.

He stands with her on a fine spring evening on the lawn of his house, overlooking Hampstead Heath.

— I don't think I should talk about these things, he says.

— Alphonse told me, she says. He said you hired him to keep an eye on her.

— He shouldn't have done that, the Baron says. It was most unprofessional of him to do that.

— He was drunk, she says

— Is he often drunk?

— When he's drunk he sings, she says. Sentimental Hungarian ballads. And accompanies himself on this creaking accordion.

— I will be terminating his contract soon, the Baron says.

— Because I told you?

— Because I'm not satisfied with him.

— Did you hire him to kill her? she asks.

— What?

— He told me he'd done jobs like that in the past, she says, and hinted that he was involved with something like that at the moment.

— My dear Isabelle! he says.

– I don't want to get caught up in that sort of thing, she says.

– Why should I want to kill her? he asks.

– How should I know? she says. Perhaps you want her dead.

– I don't like her, he says. We don't speak any more. But wanting her dead is something else.

– Why do you want to tail her?

– You know, he says, I'm not really sure. Perhaps it's just curiosity.

– Curiosity? she says.

– I'm curious to find out if she has a lover, he says.

– You should be happy if she has, she says.

– Dear Isabelle, he says. I don't know why you concern yourself with these sordid matters. They are really none of your business.

– I don't like the idea of people being killed around me, she says. And the gun being found in my luggage and all that sort of thing.

– Where do you get such ideas from? he says. They don't go with your passion for dancing.

– I won't be dancing any more if the police pin a murder on me, she says.

– You've been seeing too many films, he says. There are no guns and no one's going to get killed.

– Yes there are, she says. Alphonse has one.

– Isabelle, he says, you should get away from that man. I don't feel he's altogether reliable.

– He lets me have a free room, she says. He took me in when I needed to get away from my boyfriend.

– Is he funny? he asks.

– Funny? she says.

– I thought that might be the attraction, he says. A clown . . .

– He's an ex-clown, she says. And anyway clowns aren't funny except in public.

– He's an unsavoury character, the Baron says.

– What's unsavoury?

– Not someone you want to be mixed up with.

– That's my business, she says. I can mix with who I want. And, besides, I can't afford to rent a room.

– I could find you a little flat you could move into fairly soon, he says.

– No thanks.

– No strings attached.

– No thanks.

– You have an arrangement with him?

– Sort of.

– Affective?

– What's affective?

– Does it concern your affections?

– You mean am I sleeping with him?

– That too, he says.

– The answer is no, she says. I already told you. And you should be ashamed of yourself for asking such a question.

– Is it a business arrangement you have with him then? he asks.

– Sort of, she says.

– Then don't, he says. He's an unreliable character. Not someone you want to enter into a business arrangement with. Believe me.

– I can handle him, she says. But the gun disturbs me.

– That's what I mean, he says. He's unreliable.

– I can handle him, she says again.

– Think about my proposition, the Baron says. Purely philanthropic. No strings attached.

– There's always strings, Natasha says.

34

– When the trapeze artist falls he breaks his neck, Alphonse says, but when the clown pretends to fall he breaks the audience's heart.

– What is that supposed to mean, Alphonse? Elspeth says.

They are having lunch in one of her favourite restaurants, The March Hare, in Waterloo.

– It means that clowns are necessary whereas trapeze artists are a luxury. And why are they necessary? Because in them the audience finds the image of its own vulnerability. When your heart goes out to a clown, Alphonse says, it goes out to the sufferer in yourself, it goes out to the creature of flesh and blood whose heart breaks, whose body withers, and who soon will be no more. But we laugh at the clown, you will say, we do not cry with him. To some extent that is true. But we laugh because he has done the impossible, he has shown us our mortality and carried it away from us. The clown is our scapegoat and our guide, our servant and our master. When I tell you, Elspeth, Alphonse says, that –

She puts her hands to her ears. – I don't want to hear any more, Alphonse, she says. You are driving me mad with your words.

Elspeth lights a cigarette from the butt of the old one, and stubs the butt out fiercely in the overflowing ashtray. – I do not want to hear any more, Alphonse, she says. I want to know what is happening.

– Elspeth, he says. I have laid my plans and soon it will be done.

– I'm so confused, Alphonse, she says. I don't know whether to believe you or not.

A waiter discretely removes the overflowing ashtray and substitutes a clean one.

– It has already started, he says, smiling at her across the table.

– What has? she says.

– The frightening, he says.

– It's started? she says. What do you mean, Alphonse? Either one is frightened or one is not. One cannot start to be frightened.

– Elspeth, Elspeth, he says. Don't get yourself into a state. I tell you: It has already started.

– What did you do? she asks.

– I think the less you know about these things the better, he says. But I have begun to make my presence felt.

– Felt? she says.

– It's just the beginning, he says.

– Why didn't you tell me? she says.

– I told you, Elspeth, he says. It's all being taken care of. But you never listen to me. You are locked up in your own head, Elspeth, you really are.

– I'm so confused, Alphonse, she says. I don't know whether to believe you or not.

– Elspeth, he says, I have to go.

– Go?

– I have things to do, he says. But rest assured: I have laid my plans and soon it will be done.

– And when it is, she says, I don't want ever to see you again.

– I'm a professional man, Elspeth, he says. I always have been and I always will be.

– Do you think it'll look funny? she asks.

– What will?

– That we should cease to see each other.

– Look? he says. Look to whom?

– I don't know, she says. If it comes out I've been seeing you.

– Who will look? he says.

– But we've been seen together.

– That is all the better, he says. No one who hires someone to do what you have hired me to do is seen in their company. Never.

– That's what I mean, she says.

– Because we are seen nobody will suspect, he says. That is the beauty of it.

– But then should we not go on seeing each other afterwards?

– I'm a professional man, Alphonse says.

– I'll miss our lunches, she says.

– So will I, he says as the dessert arrives, so will I, Elspeth.

35

— Isabelle?

— Speaking.

— I thought we were going to meet?

— I'm sorry, Giles, I've been very busy.

— What about Sunday night? Helene is going to the country for a few days and I've got the house to myself. Perhaps you could come and have a meal?

— This Sunday?

— Yes.

— I'll have to think about it.

— Do you want to or not?

— I want to, Giles. But I need to think about it.

— No you don't, he says. You tell me here and now: Yes or no.

— I don't know, Giles, she says. I've got a lot on just now.

— Yes or no? he says.

— Yes. I'll come.

— I'll expect you for dinner. Seven-thirty.

— Seven-thirty.

36

— We'll take out the alarm, Lino says to his contact in Amsterdam. All you have to do is go in and get it.

He listens.

— Good, he says. Yes, he says. Sunday.

He listens.

— You should have a clear run, he says. You should be in Dover in two hours and back home in time for breakfast.

He listens.

— Yes, he says. Yes. Expect to hear from me, he says.

— Good, he says. Goodbye for now.

37

– That prick Giles has asked me to dinner on Sunday, Natasha says.

– Don't go, Rosie says.

– I don't want to go, she says. But I don't want to be rude.

– There are times when you have to be rude, Rosie says.

– I think I might go all the same.

– You'll be sorry, Rosie says.

– I like adventure, Natasha says. But he gives me the creeps.

– You can look after yourself, Rosie says. But my advice is, don't go.

– I don't know, Natasha says. I think I'll go.

38

— Isabelle?

— Hullo, Baron.

— Isabelle, is Alphonse there?

— No. I'm afraid he's out.

— Good. It's you I wanted to speak to.

— Oh yes?

— Isabelle, the Baron says, why have you vanished?

— You don't understand, Baron, Natasha says.

— Don't understand what?

— I couldn't go on seeing you, she says.

— Why not, Isabelle? I thought we got on so well.

— We do, she says.

— Then I don't understand.

— You have too much money, Baron.

— Too much money?

— Yes.

— I don't understand.

— There's too much difference between us, she says.

— In age you mean?

— There is that, she says. But it's not really the issue. The issue is that you have too much money.

— But I can't help that.

— Of course you can't, Baron. It's just one of those things.

He is silent. Then he says: I can't make you change your mind, Isabelle?

– No, she says.

– You wouldn't like to come out and dance with me again?

– I would, Baron, believe me. But I don't think it's possible.

– It pains me to hear it, he says.

– Me too, she says.

– But I can't get you to change your mind?

– No, she says.

– I see, he says.

She waits.

– I see, he says again.

– I'm sorry, Baron, she says. I enjoyed meeting you.

– And me, the Baron says. You brought light into my life, Isabelle.

– Thank you, Baron. You're a generous man.

– Goodbye then, Isabelle.

– Goodbye, Baron.

— We don't need his consent, Charlie says. We just get married.

— I can't marry without his consent, Rosie says.

— Then we don't get married.

— I suppose so, she says. Who gets married nowadays anyway?

— Will he mind?

— What?

— Us living together and not being married.

— He's broad-minded, she says. It's just that he's old-fashioned.

— Fuck him, Charlie says.

— Tash's going to have dinner with Giles on Sunday, Rosie says.

— This Sunday?

— I tried to dissuade her but that only made her more determined.

— Good, he says. You did the right thing.

— What do you mean?

— Never mind, he says.

— What are you going to do, Charlie?

— Nothing.

— Don't do anything silly.

— You know me, he says. When did I ever do anything silly?

– You're late, the Baron says.

Alphonse sits down on the bench beside him.

– You're late, the Baron says again.

– You said that already, Alphonse says.

– Well? the Baron says.

– Nothing, Alphonse says.

– Nothing at all?

– Clean as a whistle, Baron, Alphonse says.

– How long have you known her?

– Known whom?

– My wife, man, my wife.

– What do you mean, Baron?

– I ask, the Baron says, because it suddenly struck me that it might have been you I saw her with that afternoon in Soho.

– I fail to follow your line of thought, Baron, Alphonse says.

– It struck me as rather amusing, the Baron says, if that was the case.

– Why amusing?

– Work it out for yourself, the Baron says.

Alphonse is silent, contemplating the river.

– Is that it? the Baron asks.

– It, Baron?

– Investigation over?

– That is entirely up to you, Alphonse says. But my preliminary observations lead me to suspect that further probing would not reveal anything. I became acquainted with the lady, as you discovered, Baron, because that is always surer than merely tailing from a distance, and I have to say that your original observation was right. She is not interested in men, only in money. Though I detect a certain pent-up store of emotion in her, I really do.

– Pent-up store of emotion, Alphonse? the Baron says.

– I am not usually wrong in my diagnoses, Alphonse says.

The Baron pulls an envelope from his jacket pocket. – Here is the balance, he says.

Alphonse takes the envelope from him, opens it, counts the notes.

– There is the question of expenses, he says.

– That was covered by the payment, the Baron says.

– Only roughly, Alphonse says.

– Alphonse, the Baron says, I disliked you and distrusted you from the moment I set eyes on you. Everything you have done since then has only reinforced my initial impression. I think you should take what I have given you and go.

– Baron, Baron, Alphonse says, let us keep our feelings out of it. We entered into a professional agreement. I would not like to have to protect my rights.

– Are you threatening me, Alphonse? the Baron asks.

The other is silent.

– I asked if you were threatening me, the Baron says.

Alphonse sighs. – All right, Baron, he says. Let us leave it at that.

The Baron stands up. – Good day to you, he says.

Alphonse takes a packet of cigarettes out of his pocket,

selects one, puts it in his mouth and lights it. He closes his eyes and lets the smoke trickle out through his nostrils.

The Baron walks away in the direction of the London Eye.

– Papa, Rosie says, Charlie wants to invite you to the private view of his recent work. Mostly video but a few photos too.

– Are you going yourself, *cara?*

– Of course, Papa.

– Then I'll come with Mama.

– That's what Charlie hoped. He'll get the gallery to send you an invite.

– I love the movies, Lino says. I look forward to it.

– Charlie doesn't make movies, Papa.

– I know, I know, *cara*. But you know what I mean.

– OK. Bye for now, Papa.

– Listen to me, Natasha says. Just fucking listen.

– I can't believe this, Charlie says.

– You don't want to listen, she says.

– I don't believe it, he says. Some kids? On the road? I refuse to believe it.

They are sitting at a pavement table of the café in the King's Road.

– You'll have to, she says.

– There's something very strange going on, he says.

– You don't believe me? You think I'm keeping it back?

– First you find it where? he says.

– I told you, she says.

– I need to hear it again, he says.

– In the accordion, she says. It was the only thing I hadn't looked into. I should have guessed, she says, from the way he kept hugging it and the sound it was giving out.

– What do you mean? he says.

– It was sort of muffled. Not surprisingly. When I got into it there was all this paper inside. Wads and wads of it. Rolled up tight.

– So you put all this in your briefcase, he says, and you went out into the street and you handed it to a bunch of kids. I can't believe this, Tash, I can't believe what I'm hearing.

– I had my suitcase with me, she says, and my bag and this briefcase. They stopped me and asked me the way, she says.

They had this map. They opened it out and asked me the way. I put the suitcase and the briefcase down between my feet and the next thing I knew they'd pushed me over and made off with it.

— I can't believe this, he says. You didn't chase them?

— Of course I did, she says. What do you think? But they were too quick for me. And they were laughing. Not more than twelve or thirteen I'd guess. They had a head start and by the time I got to the corner they'd vanished.

— I can't believe what I'm hearing, he says.

— You'll have to, she says.

— All this time, he says. All this effort. And finally you find it and . . . No, he says, I just don't believe it.

— You think I'm keeping it back?

He looks at her. — No, he says. It's not your way, Tash.

— I should fucking think not, she says.

— I still can't believe it, he says.

— Somebody's going to get a nice surprise, she says.

— I hope you had fun anyway, he says.

— It was interesting, she says.

They gaze out at the crowds surging past on this warm spring morning.

— So this is it, he says.

— Uhuh.

— And what are you going to do with yourself now, Tash?

— I have plans.

— You're going back to him?

— Who him?

— The clown.

— What do you think I'm carrying this suitcase for? she says. Besides, mission's accomplished, I wouldn't want to stay on.

– What about Giles?

– Just shut the fuck up, she says.

– You're seeing him on Sunday, aren't you?

– Who told you that?

– Rosie.

– I told her I didn't want her to talk about me, she says.
Shit.

They gaze at the crowds surging past.

– You could come back to me, he says.

– No thanks. Anyway, you're with Rosie now.

– Sure. But you could come back to me.

– No thanks. Rosie's my friend.

– OK then.

– See you then.

– See you.

43

— I've been so worried, Elspeth says. I've been ringing you non-stop, Alphonse. Why do you carry a mobile if it's always switched off?

— Is it, Elspeth? he says.

— Of course it is, she says. I've been trying to get you for the past week, Alphonse. I've been so worried in case you did something.

— Did something, Elspeth?

— Alphonse, she says, were you responsible for that burglary?

— What burglary, Elspeth?

— You know Giles has had his Braque stolen?

— I heard about it.

— You didn't see it on the news?

— I saw it, he says.

— And you weren't involved?

— Me? Why should I be? I had my own burglary here.

— Here? What are you talking about, Alphonse?

— That woman made off with my money.

— Alphonse, she says, what's happening to everything? First there was the robbery and now the Baron has disappeared and left me a note saying he forgives me for everything and I don't know where I am any more.

— You never knew where you were before, Elspeth, he says. You really didn't.

— Oh, Alphonse, she says, this isn't the time for that sort of remark. Can I see you, Alphonse? There's so much to talk about.

— Only if you come here.

— Here? To your flat?

— Yes.

— Why?

— I've done something to my foot, Elspeth. I'm in bed and have no one to look after me.

— Isn't that frightful girl there?

— No, he says. She moved out. She burgled me and moved out.

— Moved? Where to?

— She's disappeared, Elspeth. That's what I'm trying to tell you.

— What happened to your foot, Alphonse?

There is a silence.

— I got a bullet in it, he says at last. That's what happened.

— A bullet? she says. I don't understand what you're saying, Alphonse. Has someone been shooting at you?

— Yes, Alphonse says.

— But why? she says. What happened? Were you drunk, Alphonse? You were involved in that burglary, weren't you? I knew it, she says. The police have sealed all the airports. It was insured of course, but it's irreplaceable. Of course, she says, the thieves won't be able to sell it, but they're probably working for a private Japanese collector anyway. Helene's in hospital, Alphonse. She seems to have suffered a shock but the baby's all right. She's called Olivia. Olivia Matilda.

— What baby? he says. I wish you'd be more coherent, Elspeth.

– The baby she was expecting, she says. The shock led to a premature birth but Olivia's all right.

– All right? he says.

– That's why it was so urgent to get hold of you. The Baron has left me a generous annuity and Felix's cottage. For some reason he's given Felix the house. So thank God you took so long to act. Thank God for that. Alphonse, are you there?

– Yes, Elspeth, I'm here.

– Alphonse, she says, did you think something like this might happen? Was that why you didn't act?

– I told you I had everything under control, Elspeth, didn't I?

– Did you arrange it with the Baron? she says. Did you arrange for him to change his will and leave me my annuity?

He is silent.

– Alphonse, she says, who shot you in the foot?

– It was an accident, he says.

– An accident? I thought you said someone shot you?

There is a silence.

– Alphonse, she says, there's something I don't understand about all this. Why has the Baron disappeared and left all his possessions behind? Alphonse, he took my hammock away and left me Felix's cottage and an annuity. Are you behind this, Alphonse?

He is silent.

– Alphonse, she says, are you there?

– Yes, Elspeth, he says.

– What's all this about an accident, Alphonse?

– It's a long story, Elspeth, it really is.

– Can't we meet and talk about it, Alphonse? I don't know how I'm going to manage because Felix seems to have disappeared as well. The Baron says in his letter that he's left him the house, but he's gone too as far as I can see. I'm afraid, the Baron says, and I'm quoting his very words, I'm afraid you'll no longer be able to retain the services of Felix. What does that mean, Alphonse?

– It means what it says, Elspeth. It really does.

– I could come and cook for you, Alphonse, she says. If you give me the address. I used to be quite a good cook once, before the Baron corrupted me with his wealth. Then you could explain it all to me. Is that a good idea?

– Only if you want to, Elspeth.

– The police suspect an international gang, she says. They're keeping watch on all the airports but of course they could have got away the very night they did it. They tied Giles up and left him in the pantry. It was only when the cleaning lady got in the next day that she found him. Helene was in hospital with the baby, recovering, but he'd cooked a meal for two and laid out the best crockery and silver, but now he says he can't remember a thing. Do you believe that, Alphonse, that someone could lose their memory like that? After laying the table for two when he knew very well Helene was in hospital with the baby, recovering?

– Didn't he see them, Elspeth?

– He can't remember, she says. He can't remember anything about that evening. He can't remember laying the table for two or preparing a meal for two and he can't remember anyone getting in and tying him up. Who shot you in the foot, Alphonse?

– Elspeth, he says, you are working yourself up, you really

are. Come and make me some supper and we'll talk about it all.

— What does he mean, Alphonse, that he's leaving me Felix's cottage? One minute he's cutting me out of his will and leaving all his money to Giles and Helene and setting detectives on my tail and the next he forgives me everything and leaves me an annuity and Felix's cottage. Do you know what he's up to, Alphonse?

— No, Alphonse says. I really don't.

— I thought you were working for him, Alphonse?

— That came to an end some time ago, Alphonse says.

— Do you have any idea where he is, Alphonse? she asks.

— No, Alphonse says.

— Oh, Alphonse, she says, I'm so confused. I'm smoking about three packets a day and my throat feels like sandpaper.

— You shouldn't do that, Elspeth, he says. You really shouldn't.

— I should never have hired you, she says. I should never have gone down that road. Thank goodness nothing came of it, Alphonse.

— We have to live by our decisions, Elspeth, he says. We really do.

— What does that mean? she says.

There is a silence.

— You do agree with me, Alphonse, don't you? she says. I knew it was unwise the moment I did it. My cigarette intake doubled the moment I got in touch with you. That should have been a sign to me, Alphonse, shouldn't it?

— Elspeth, he says, I'm going to put the phone down. I can't take any more of this. I really can't.

— I'm sorry, Alphonse, she says, but you have to see it from my point of view. Am I a rich woman or aren't I? Has he gone off with another woman or hasn't he? Is Felix in on this or isn't he? Are you in his pay or mine? Can you see it from my point of view, Alphonse?

– I can't take any more of this, Elspeth, he says. I really can't. Are you going to come and cook me a meal or aren't you?

– Of course I am, she says. If you give me the address I'll be there as soon as I can.

– Just this evening, Elspeth, he says. I need to rest during the day.

– I won't disturb you, she says. Have you been to the doctor about your foot?

– I can't move, Elspeth, he says. I'm holed up in bed here and I can't move.

– You can get the doctor to come and see you, she says. Even in this day and age they still do if you insist enough.

– And have him ask me questions about the bullet? he says.

– What happened, Alphonse? she asks. You haven't told me what happened.

– I'll tell you, Elspeth, he says. Just come round this evening and I'll tell you all about it.

– I'm so worried, she says. What does he mean he's left me an annuity of fifty thousand pounds? Does he think he can buy my silence at that price? Or is he playing one of his games with me?

– You have to see a solicitor, Elspeth, Alphonse says. You have to see your solicitor and get it all straightened out.

– I'm seeing him tomorrow, she says. Apparently the Baron left him instructions as well. But perhaps there's a catch in it.

Why should he leave the house to Felix? Why does he want to humiliate me by leaving me Felix's cottage?

    – This is the address, Alphonse says. Have you got a pencil and paper?

44

– I had hoped Mr O'Hagan would say a few words about his work, says Miles Quilligan, the gallery owner, after the crowd of guests has at last grown silent, but for understandable reasons he has declined. Instead, I am happy to say, the distinguished critic, Hector Zamora, has agreed to step into the breach and introduce the work you see around you.

The distinguished critic, large, imposing, black hair about his shoulders, stands up. – Wallace Stevens, the American poet, he begins, once wrote a little poem called 'A Jar in Tenessee'. That poem tells how a landscape is given focus and meaning by the placing of a jar in its midst. The title of this show, *Ajar*, is perhaps a witty reflection on that poem and its subject. For the photos you see on the walls and the videos you can watch on the two monitors, are all about the transition from the meaningless to the meaningful, the raw to the cooked, nature to culture, and about the transition back again. About the loss this often entails and the gains that sometimes ensue. Most artists, continues Zamora, are content to explore the one or the other, nature or culture, and a few very great artists have explored both. What is striking about the work you see around you is that it explores not the one state or the other but the nature of the boundary between them and the nature of the transition from the one to the other. It does this not through the heightened rhetoric of expressionism or the cool rhetoric of pop, but through a kind of absence – an absence of style, an absence of 'voice'. One can see this most clearly in the series of videos the artist has made of doors.

He pauses and, taking out his handkerchief, mops his brow, for the crush in the little gallery has sent the temperature soaring. – What is a door? he goes on in his commanding voice. As the Romans knew, a door is a two-faced thing, a Janus. Closed, it is mere surface, a part of the façade if the door is a front door, as most of these are. Open, it is a conduit, a passage from inner to outer and from outer to inner. An open door is in a sense a door no longer. It has vanished and in its place is a gap, a place of darkness, of negativity, before which we wait in expectation.

He pauses again and sweeps his arms round the room. – You will see, on the walls here, he goes on, photographs of open doors and also photographs of doors in various stages of openness and closedness. But there is no drama here, as in Kafka's parable of the door and its keeper. No allegory. These remain ordinary doors in ordinary houses and the people who go in and out of them remain ordinary people. Sometimes they wave to the camera as they go in, half turning as they do so, acknowledging the presence of the photographer; sometimes they wave as they come out, emerging from the dark into the light. Most of the time they seem unaware, simply living their lives, going about their ordinary business.

– So much, says Zamora, mopping his brow and neck with his now sopping handkerchief, for the photographs on the walls. However, the most interesting work in the show is, to my mind, the video work. Here, it seems to me, the artist comes fully into his own, his subject matter finds its rightful medium. Once again the subject at its simplest is doors. The camera remains steady for several minutes, and, since nothing moves, we could be looking at a photograph. But wait. Suddenly the smooth façade is disturbed. A line of darkness appears. A door is starting to open. It remains ajar for a long time, and once more we settle to look at a photograph, only this time of a white wall with a portion taken out of it, or a white façade with a black vertical cutting into it. Or the door is pulled quite open and a figure appears, its back towards us, slowly leaving the interior before turning on the step. Or a figure appears on the step, its back towards us, crouches, inserts a key into the door, opens the door, straightens, enters, closes the door again. Or the door opens from the inside and a figure stands for a moment on the threshold, looking out, turns round, closes the door, turns again and hurries out of shot. This particular sequence, this subtle combination of stillness and movement, reminds me of the work of another video artist, Tacita Dean. In one of her videos Dean focuses on a sheet of water beyond which can be seen the giant form of a disused sonar station. Nothing moves. The walls stand still, the dark water in the foreground is still, the camera is still. We could be looking at a rather beautifully composed photograph. And then we notice that the water is in fact not still, that it is moving steadily from the right to the left of the screen. But the movement is so minimal that it takes us a while to realise that it is happening at all. And though the motion is so steady as to be almost another kind of stillness, it is the kind of stillness that can only be caught by a movie or video camera.

– In the case of the work we have here, Zamora goes on, the effect is less minimal, more human. We are, after all, in a city, not out in the countryside. Houses are built by people, for people. Nevertheless, there are parallels. We see a door, set in a façade, for several minutes. We become habituated to it. Then there is movement. The door swings inward, a block of darkness invests the screen, a figure emerges, the door is shut again and once more there is stillness. Have our eyes deceived us? Did anything in fact happen? What has intruded into our consciousness, Zamora says, is time, pure time. Without the opening of the door and its reshutting, time would have stood still. And it seems to stand still. But the image is haunted by *what happened*, and therefore may happen again. The basic elements of drama have emerged: suspense, our eagerness to know *what happens next*. Such an effect, he goes on, can even be achieved with a single image. The image of a door ajar, which appears several times on these walls, is the image, precisely, of suspense, of waiting for an *advent*. That is why I would venture to say that these apparently secular, urban, uneventful images are in fact images which belong squarely to the religious tradition of the West, images which link the artist with a long line of Catholic painters who have sought in their art to capture the mystery of incarnation, of the existence or appearance of the divine in our midst, its presence amongst the most banal and humdrum elements of life. But I have spoken for long enough. As the Americans say, enjoy!

Rosie turns to her father. – What did you think, Papa?

– I had no idea, Lino says.

– No idea of what?

– It just looked like doors to me. Now he says it's Catholic and religious.

– You want to have a look?

They get up and go over to one of the monitors. A group of people with glasses in their hands have gathered round it. Lino sits in the last free chair. Rosie stands behind him, her hands on the back of the chair. The video has already started. The screen is mainly taken up by sky, seen from the inside of a moving car. Occasionally the tops of buildings lurch drunkenly into view and, as the sky darkens, streetlights punctuate the sky. The end arrives abruptly.

– An early work, Rosie says.

The second video is almost static, the camera facing a door which slowly opens from the inside to reveal a dark interior. Then the door slowly closes again.

– Part of the effect comes from the silence, someone says. Imagine a movie of this, how the music would ruin it.

The third follows a ball as it rolls down a path and eventually comes to rest at the edge of a pond filled with lilies.

– Another early work, Rosie says.

– *Cara,* Lino says. I have to go home. Mama is waiting.

But the fourth video has already begun. Once again the camera faces a door, but this time it is recognisably the front door of a smart house, reached by means of a short flight of steps and enclosed in a porch. Suddenly a man enters the frame, seen from the back. He looks round furtively and the audience gathered about the monitor gasps, for the man's face is covered by a black balaclava helmet, made familiar from images of IRA and other terrorists. At once the gasps turn to laughter as a second man, his face also covered by a balaclava, joins the first and the two struggle with the door until it abruptly opens and they disappear inside. The door closes again. The minutes tick by. The audience chat and joke among themselves. Then the door on the screen opens again abruptly and one of the men steps out, walking slowly backwards. He is holding a large oblong object, covered in a black cloth. The second man emerges and the two stand for

[148]

a second on the porch, balancing the object between them as the second man pulls the door shut. Then they slowly move out of shot, the first man shuffling slowly backwards, then the covered object, then the second man. There is another minute of the porch and the closed door and the video comes to an end.

The audience drifts away.

– I hadn't seen that, Rosie says.

Lino is silent.

– You need to see them several times, she says. You need to enter their rhythm.

The sequence begins again. A new group forms round the monitor. Charlie strolls over to them. – Come and have a drink, he says.

– You stay, *cara,* Lino says, standing up. I'm going home.

– Are you feeling all right, Papa?

– Of course. You stay.

– It was good of him to come, Charlie says as they watch him leave the gallery.

– Oh, he wanted to come, Rosie says. He's interested in your work.

– You think he liked it?

– *I* liked it, she says. I hadn't seen the last one.

– It's a new direction, he says. Zamora hadn't seen it of course. It throws his naff comments right out of the window.

– I liked what he said, Rosie says.

– Naff, Charlie says. But there's critics for you.

45

Elspeth finishes bathing Alphonse's foot and begins to bandage it.

– Felix has gone, she says. Only Wally the gardener is left. I'm beginning to enjoy myself alone there, but it's a pity about the hammock.

– I can see you're enjoying yourself, Alphonse says. You're not smoking so much and your skin looks healthier.

– My skin was always healthy, Elspeth says. And I wouldn't smoke here with you sick and everything anyway.

– You would have before, Alphonse says. You really would.

– That's true, she says. Perhaps I would. There, she says, how does that feel?

– All right, he says grudgingly.

– Now, she says, you can perhaps tell me what happened.

– I was standing in the garden, Alphonse says. Where I'd stood before, when I went the first time. Behind that tree. I heard her moving in the house and waited for her to come out, as I knew she would, eventually. I had the gun ready and when the light came on in the kitchen I raised it and took aim at the door.

– You were going to shoot her? she says, horrified.

– Of course, he says. Except it was my clown's gun, which only shoots flowers.

– It wasn't loaded?

– Only joking, he says.

– So you *were* going to shoot her?

– Elspeth, he says, will you let me tell the story or won't you?

– I'm sorry, she says.

– I had the gun ready and when the light came on in the kitchen, he says, I raised it and took aim at the door. I watched it slowly open and then she stood there, looking straight out at me, bathed in light. I raised my arm and she saw the gun and her hand went up to her mouth and at that moment something fell on me out of that tree and the gun went off and she screamed and I felt this terrible pain in my foot and in my neck. The creature that had jumped on me ran off, screeching, she fell back into the room, and I took off. I don't know how I got here. I must have passed out a couple of times on the Tube, but I made it. I was sure I'd shot my foot off, but when I removed my shoe I found the bullet had only scraped the bone.

– You were going to kill her?

– That's what you asked me to do, he says.

– Well, it's lucky you didn't, she says. Now the Baron has left me all this money without my having to do anything.

– I told you these things shouldn't be rushed, Alphonse says. But you pressed and pressed.

– How was I to know it would turn out like this? she says. Luckily it was only shock and Helene is recovering in hospital, having given birth to a bonny girl, who is fine herself, and even that swine Giles has recovered from his ordeal.

– Now there is the question of the rest of my fee, he says.

– But you didn't do it, she says.

– I did my best, Elspeth, he says. And it turned out for the best. It really did.

[151]

– Do you drive a car? she asks him.

– Me? he says. Of course. Why?

– The Baron has left me the car, she says. And Felix has vanished. Though even if he was still there I don't suppose he'd be willing to drive me around any more now that he has the big house. You could come and live with me, she says. The cottage isn't very big but I'm sure we could manage.

Alphonse stares at his bandaged foot.

– Do you want to think about it? she asks.

– Now Isabelle has left this place seems pretty desolate, he says. She was a big girl and she's left a big gap. I don't see why I shouldn't accept your offer, Elspeth, I really don't.

46

– *Cara,* it's Papa. I want to speak to Charlie.

– To Charlie?

– He's with you?

– Yes, Papa, but why do you want to speak to him?

– Let me speak to him, *cara*.

– It's Papa, she says, covering the phone. He wants to speak to you.

– Yes? Charlie says, picking up the phone.

– What's this film about, eh? Lino says.

– What film?

– You go to the police?

– The police? I'm an artist, Lino. The police can do their own dirty work.

– You go to the papers?

– What's this about, Lino?

– How much? Lino says.

– How much what?

– How much you want?

– For the photos?

– The lot.

– What lot?

– Charlie, Lino says. Don't fool with me. Ten thou.

– Ten thousand?

– You want more?

– Rosie wants us to get married.

– That's a good idea, Charlie. Why you no ask me?

– She's asked you, Lino. You said not on your life, because I was an artist.

– That was before I saw the film, Lino says.

There is a silence.

– Make it fifteen thousand and you marry her, Lino says. Everything, all copies, all negatives, everything.

– Fifteen thousand?

– Yes.

– Why the change of heart? Charlie says.

– I like your work, Lino says. For fifteen thou I buy everything, you understand? Everything. And you make new photos of the restaurant, OK?

– Hey, Charlie says, hold on. I have to think about this.

– OK, Lino says. Fifteen thou just for the videos. And a written guarantee they are my exclusive property.

– Twenty, Charlie says.

– Fifteen, Lino says.

– I'll settle for eighteen, Charlie says.

– Done, Lino says. You give Rosie the videos and she bring them to me and I give you the eighteen and my blessing. OK?

– Lino, Charlie says, you're a sweet man. I always thought so.

– I don't know about sweet, Lino says. But I run the best restaurant in Knightsbridge.

– You do, Lino, you do.

– You don't fool with me, eh, Charlie? Lino says. You give her the videos and all the film you have and she bring them to me and I give you eighteen thou and my blessing.

– It's a deal, Charlie says.

[154]

He puts down the phone. — Your father's become an art collector, he says.

— What do you mean?

He explains the deal to her.

— He's got a good heart, she says. And a good brain too. He senses your work's about to take off and he knows a good thing when he sees one.

— He wants us to get married, Charlie says.

— I thought he'd come round to it, she says, when he recognised the quality of your work. A good heart and a good business brain, that's him.

— Both of which qualities you have inherited, my darling, Charlie says, and lifts her off the ground.

47

Natasha and the Baron sit sipping ouzo in a café high up above the bay of Symi, a Greek island close to the Turkish coast of Asia Minor.

– I loved his body, Natasha says, but he had the mind of a flea. Besides, I couldn't stand his arrogance.

– I'm quite arrogant myself, the Baron says.

– Nothing like Charlie, she says. And I love your body even more than his.

– I don't think you should make those sorts of comparisons, the Baron says.

– Oh don't be so prissy, she says.

In the square above them a Greek popular song is blaring through the loudspeakers. It is interrupted by a high-pitched whine and the song splutters to a stop. It starts up again, briefly, stops again. A voice says something in Greek.

– What was that? Natasha asks.

– I didn't catch. Let's go up and see.

Leaving their things at the café table they climb the few steps to the square. A booth has been set up at one end and two young people in jeans and long hair are taking things out of a box and hanging them on pegs behind the booth. Rows of chairs have been arranged in the square to face the booth and groups of excited children have already taken their places, laughing and talking. Further back, on benches round the perimeter of the square, a few adults sit chatting or merely resting, their shopping bags at their feet.

The Baron goes up to the two youths and has a word with them. Natasha sits down at the end of an empty row of chairs and looks up at the cloudless sky, now slowly darkening.

The Baron leaves the booth and comes and stands beside her. He lays a hand on her glossy hair and she, without moving her head, puts her hand on his.

– It's Karagoz, he says. The shadow puppet play. The performance begins at nine.

She strokes his hand.

– It's Turkish, he says. It's good to see it being done here.

– Don't lecture me, please, she says.

– I'm sorry.

– No, she says. *I'm* sorry.

From the square the hills are visible, bare now of the forests which once covered them but were all in time cut down to build the Turkish fleets.

They return to the café and order another ouzo.

– Natasha, he says.

She looks at him. – How did you know? she says.

– I looked at your passport.

– I'm glad, she says.

– Glad?

– I hated that name.

– It was a beautiful name, he says.

– It wasn't mine, she says.

– True, he says.

– You're a one to talk, she says.

– What do you mean?

– You're not a Baron at all.

– I never said I was. It's just what people call me.

– It doesn't matter what you're called, she says. You're still you. And what's that telegram in your passport about?

– It's from Felix, he says.

– I saw it was from Felix, she says. What does it mean, Yolande new Miss Jenkin 764152?

– She was my nanny, he says. I loved her dearly.

– What does it mean, new Miss Jenkin?

– It's code, he says. It means everything has worked out as I hoped it would. Elspeth has moved to the cottage with Alphonse and Felix is travelling round the world.

He puts a hand on hers. – Natasha, he says, after Karagoz we could go dancing if you liked?

– I'd like, she says, and laughs.

Ⓑ *editions*